saving francesca

melina marchetta

saving francesca

alfred a. knopf

new york

THIS IS A BORZOI BOOK PUBLISHED BY ALFRED A. KNOPF

All rights reserved. Published in the United States by Alfred A. Knopf, an imprint
of Random House Children's Books, a division of Random House, Inc., New York.
Originally published in paperback in Australia by Viking Children's Books, a division
of Penguin Books Australia, Camberwell, in 2003, and subsequently published in
hardcover in the United States by Alfred A. Knopf in 2004.

Knopf, Borzoi Books, and the colophon are registered trademarks of Random House, Inc.

Visit us on the Web! www.randomhouse.com/teens

Educators and librarians, for a variety of teaching tools, visit us at
www.randomhouse.com/teachers

The Library of Congress has cataloged the hardcover edition of this work as follows:
Marchetta, Melina.
Saving Francesca / Melina Marchetta.
p.   cm.
Summary: Sixteen-year-old Francesca could use her outspoken mother's help
with the problems of being one of a handful of girls at a parochial school
that has just turned coed, but her mother has suddenly become severely depressed.
ISBN 978-0-375-82982-6 (trade) — ISBN 978-0-375-92982-3 (lib. bdg.) —
ISBN 978-0-307-43371-8 (ebook)
[1. Sexism—Fiction. 2. Catholic schools—Fiction. 3. Schools—Fiction. 4. Depression,
Mental—Fiction. 5. Family life—Australia—Fiction. 6. Sydney (N.S.W.)—Fiction.
7. Australia—Fiction.] I. Title.
PZ7.M32855Sav 2004
[Fic]—dc22
2004003926

ISBN 978-0-375-82983-3 (tr. pbk.)

Printed in the United States of America
10 9 8 7 6 5 4 3 2 1

ACKNOWLEDGMENTS

Mum, Dad, Marisa, Daniela—thanks for the whole Grand Central Station experience.

To my mum, Christine Alesich, Barbara Barclay, Marcus Burnett, Anthony Douglas, Philippa Gibson, Laura Harris, Damian Hatton, Janet Hill, Sophia Hill, Genevieve and Olivia Hill (for typing out your mum's notes), Brenda Hokin, Annette Hughes, Brother Eric Hyde, David McGuigan, Michelle Patane, Mark Roppolo, Aaron Taranto (and Wade, although you weren't supposed to read it), Francus Vierboom, Julie Watts, Kate Woods, Maxim Younger, and Toby Younger. Thanks for your advice about the manuscript or for writing ten pages of notes for me or feeding my ego or inspiring me with your own writing or pointing out the difference between a pipeline and a grind pole.

Thanks also to Beth Yahp, Teresa Crea, and Agnes Nieuwenhuizen for giving me the opportunity to create fragments of Francesca over the past ten years in your anthologies and performance piece.

For Luca

and

the St. Mary's Cathedral College boys

. . . and for the girls there, too . . .

Chapter 1

THIS MORNING, MY mother didn't get out of bed.

It meant I didn't have to go through one of her daily pep talks, which usually begin with a song that she puts on at 6:45 every morning. It's mostly seventies and eighties retro crap, anything from "I Will Survive" to some woman called Kate Bush singing, "Don't give up." When I question her choices, she says they're random, but I know that they are subliminal techniques designed to motivate me into being just like her.

But this morning there is no song. There is no advice on how to make friends with the bold and the interesting. No twelve-point plan on the best way to make a name for myself in a hostile environment. No motivational messages stuck on my mirror urging me to do something that scares me every day.

There's just silence.

And for the first time all year, I go to school and my only agenda is to get to 3:15.

***

School is St. Sebastian's in the city. It's a predominantly all-boys school that has opened its doors to girls in Year Eleven for the first time ever. My old school, St. Stella's, only goes to Year Ten and most of my friends now go to Pius Senior College, but my mother wouldn't allow it because she says the girls there leave with limited options and she didn't bring me up to have limitations placed upon me. If you know my mother, you'll sense there's an irony there, based on the fact that she is the Queen of the Limitation Placers in my life. My brother, Luca, is in Year Five at Sebastian's, so my mother figured it would be convenient for all of us in the long run, and my dad goes along with it because no one in my family has ever pretended that my mother doesn't make all the decisions.

There are thirty of us girls at Sebastian's and I want so much not to do the teenage angst thing, but I have to tell you that I hate the life that, according to my mother, I'm not actually having.

It's like this. Girls just don't belong at St. Sebastian's. We belong in schools that were built especially for us, or in co-ed schools. St. Sebastian's pretends it's co-ed by giving us our own toilet. The rest of the place is all male and I know what you're thinking if you're a girl. What a dream come true, right? Seven hundred and fifty boys and thirty girls? But the reality is that it's either like living in a fish-bowl or like you don't exist. Then, on top of that, you have to make a whole new group of friends after being in a comfortable little niche for four years. At Stella's, you turned up at school, knew exactly what your group's role and profile was, and the day was a blend of all you found comfortable. My mother calls that compla-cency but whatever it's called, I miss it like hell.

Here, at Sebastian's, after a term of being together, the girls haven't really moved on in the sorority department. I don't exactly have friends as much as ex–Stella girls I hang around with who I had barely exchanged a word with over the last four years. Justine Kalinsky, for example, came to Stella's in Year Eight and never actually seemed to make any friends there. She plays the piano accordion. There's also Siobhan Sullivan, who uses us as a disembarkation point for when one of the guys calls her over. In Year Seven, for a term, Siobhan and I were the most hysterical of friends because we were the only ones who wanted to gallop around the playground like horses while the rest of the Stella girls sat around in semicircles being young ladies. Most of our free time was spent making up dance moves to Kylie songs in our bedrooms and performing them in the playground until someone pointed out that we were showing off. My group found me just after that, thank God, and I never really spoke to Siobhan Sullivan again. My friends always told me they wanted to rescue me from Siobhan, and I relished being saved because it meant that people stopped tapping me on the shoulder to point out what I was doing wrong.

Tara Finke hangs out with us as well. She was the resident Stella psycho, full of feminist, communist, anythingist rhetoric, and if there is one thing I've noticed around here, it's that Sebastian boys don't like speeches. Especially not from us girls. They'd actually be very happy if we never opened our mouths at all. Tara's already been called a lesbian because that's how the Sebastian boys deal with any girl who has an opinion, and because there are only four ex–Stella girls, I assume the rest of us get called the same thing. I could get all politically correct here and say that there's nothing wrong with being called a lesbian, but it all comes down to being labeled something that you're not. Tara Finke thinks she's going to be able to set up a women's movement at the school, but girls run for miles when they see her coming.

The girls from St. Perpetua's, another Year Seven to Ten school, make up the bulk of the female students. They don't want to get involved with Tara and her movement because their mothers have taught them to go with the flow, which I personally think is the best advice anyone can get. My mother is a different story. She's a communications lecturer at the University of Technology–Sydney, and her students think she's the coolest thing around. But they don't have to put up with her outbursts or her inability to let anything go. If it's not an argument with the guy at the bank who pushed in front of us, it'll be questioning the rude tone of some service-industry person over the phone. She's complained to personnel at our local supermarket so many times about the service that I'm sure they have photos of my family at the door with instructions to never let us in.

Every day I come home from St. Sebastian's and my mother asks me if I've addressed the issue of the toilets, or the situation with subject selection or girls' sports. Or if I've made new friends, or if there's a guy there that I'm interested in. And every afternoon I mumble a "no" and she looks at me with great disappointment and says, "Frankie, what happened to the little girl who sang 'Dancing Queen' at the Year Six graduation night?" I'm not quite sure what wearing a white pants suit and boots, belting out an Abba hit, has to do with liberating the girls of St. Sebastian's, but somehow my mother makes the connection.

4

So I come home ready to mumble my "no" again. Ready for the look, the lecture, the unexpected analogies and the disappointment.

But she's still in bed.

Luca and I wait for my dad at the front door because my mother never stays in bed, even if she has a temperature over 104 degrees. But today the Mia we all know disappears and she becomes someone with nothing to say.

Someone a bit like me.

Chapter 2

I WAKE UP to silence. No songs about surviving. No songs about boots meant for walking. And then, after a moment, I hear her being sick in the bathroom. For a moment I'm relieved because there is a symptom. I wonder if she could be pregnant, but it's too strange a thought. She's only been at the university for over a year, and she worked hard for so long to get the position. Mia would have been careful about jeopardizing that.

Later, when I get out of bed, my dad is in the kitchen and he looks at me and tries to force a smile. My dad's a builder and I love that about him. His name is Robert and my mum calls him Bob the Builder. They've known each other since they were my age, so they're kind of like best friends. He's a bit immature, and I know that some of my mum's friends think she should have outgrown him years ago. Some of his friends joke around that he should never have let her go and get her masters, as if the control was all his. It's what I love about Bob the Builder. He doesn't give a damn what his friends or family say. He doesn't give a damn that his wife has a dozen more degrees than he ever will. He works for himself, refusing to expand because he reckons it will change everything. I think my dad just likes what he does and who he is. Sometimes my mum and her friends ask each other what they'd do if they had another life. My dad's answer is always the same. He'd marry a girl called Mia and they'd have two kids.

Whatever this thing is with my mum, I don't think it's cancer or anything, and it certainly isn't pregnancy, because my dad would probably be ecstatic about that. Today he just looks tired and confused.

"Is she okay?" I ask.

"She's just a bit down. Go get Luca out of bed."

I'm not quite sure what "just a bit down" means. I'm "just a lot down" and I'm getting out of bed.

"Did you have a fight or something?"

They are eternal arguers. She is the Queen of Hypotheticals and he's the master of not thinking beyond the next moment. She believes that if she doesn't challenge what they stand for, they'll end up like other couples they know.

"Take away your job and take away your kids and who are you, Robert?" she asked once, over dinner.

"Your husband," he said, in what she calls his droll voice.

"Then take away me and who are you?"

"Take away you, the kids, and my job? Is this a trick question? I'm dead, right?" He asked, "What are *you* if we take away all those things, Mia? Can *you* be you without all of us?"

Luca was looking from one to the other.

"Must you talk about this in front of the children?" I asked.

"You think too much and you analyze too much," he'd tell her. "Everything's fine. The kids are happy. We're happy. Everything's fine."

Mia would do that a lot last year. Analyze stuff to bits, contemplate the meaning of life. My nonno had died suddenly the year before. One minute he was watering his garden, next minute he was dead from an aneurysm. "A piece of me is gone," she told me once while we were bra shopping. "I think we're made up of all these different pieces and every time someone goes, you're left with less of yourself."

A woman with a big bust had my breasts cupped in her hands at the time, so I wasn't much in the mood for a philosophical discussion and I didn't respond. I do that a lot. Even if she asks me a great question. It shits me that she can keep me interested. Most of the time she's right about me and what I'm all about, but once, *just once,* I'd like to come up with a Francesca theory before her.

"Eggs?"

My father holds two eggs in his hands and I'm back to reality. I don't eat eggs. Nor does Luca. But I don't have the heart to tell him that.

Later, Luca and I go into their bedroom to say goodbye. She looks tiny, huddled under the blankets. Sometimes I forget how small she is because she is so vocal. She's kind of like a dynamo who does one thousand things at once, successfully. This new Mia, I don't know. She looks sick and helpless and, worse still, vulnerable. As we walk out, she stirs but she doesn't even look at us.

I go to school with a sick feeling in my stomach, and I dare not look at my brother's face because I know that I'll see on his what he can see on mine.

Tara Finke corners me as soon as I step into homeroom.

"Today's the day," she says, waving over one of the ex–Perpetua girls, who chooses to ignore her.

She tries to grab Siobhan Sullivan as she's walking in. "Are you with us or not?"

Siobhan Sullivan doesn't even bother stopping. There's some loser on the other side of the room that she has to impress.

"I wouldn't rely on Francesca either," Siobhan says over her shoulder, with a trace of spite in her voice.

I've noticed since the beginning of the year that if she ever has to make reference to me, the comments are snide, and I feel like retaliating. But that would mean I actually care what she thinks. Siobhan's nickname used to be the Slut of St. Stella's, thought up by someone inspired by an alliteration lesson in Year Nine. A mean part of me would like to pass that on, except I think everyone here is already working it out for themselves.

I sit at my desk and watch Tara organizing the ex–Perpetua girls.

"We're having House meetings this afternoon. It's time to tell them what we think of this place."

"What's wrong with it?" Eva Rodriguez asks. The ex–Perpetua girls tend to follow Eva around like she's their security blanket. She's so effortlessly cool and protective of her lot, and most of the time I wish I were one of them.

"The invasion of our personal space," Tara Finke answers, invading Eva Rodriguez's personal space. "No girls' sports offered, and when we do PE we have to share three toilets to get changed or do it out in the open. Or the fact that you can't use the words 'oral task' or 'penalized' or the number 69 without a guy in your class snickering loudly and grunting. Ring a bell, girls?"

The bell rings, thank God.

"Or that some of the girls get wolf-whistled," she says, following them to their seats, "and others get called dogs. Or that we actually came to this place because of its drama department and this year they decide to put on *Stalag 17,* which has not one female role, or that some teachers insist on addressing the class as—"

"Gentlemen, get to your seats, please," Mr. Brolin orders.

Eva Rodriguez looks at Tara Finke and then at me. "Let's just learn to live with it."

I nod. Things could be worse.

Thomas Mackee enters the class and burps into my ear.

Thomas Mackee is a perfect example of most of the boys in my homeroom. They have nicknames like Booger and Jabber and they wear those names with pride. Sometimes they attempt a bit of irony—for example, calling a guy who's absolutely clueless "Einstein." But other times it's obvious—the guy with the lowest intelligence level I've ever come across is called "Duh-Brain." Most of the nicer guys have girlfriends, and we know this because they make it clear the moment we're introduced, as if to say, "Don't think about it." Those particular guys have absolutely no idea what to do with girls who aren't girlfriends, so at the moment they're at a bit of a dead loss in the friendship department. The smarter ones feel slightly threatened, thanks to all the media coverage about girls dominating in the classroom, and they make sure that we don't take their seats at the front.

Tara Finke's theory about Thomas Mackee is that he was dropped a few times on his head as a baby. He's the poster boy for Slobs Inc.: shirt out, pants around the thighs, and brightly colored boxer shorts that are completely obvious every time he bends down, which is quite often. I'm sure he spends copious amounts of time in front of the mirror trying to get that slept-on, feral look, popular with the surfers and skateboarders at Sebastian's. He's watched a few too many *Bill & Ted's Excellent Adventure* films and likes saying things like "Hey, dude, what's happening?" in a deadpan voice. He's cruel as well. Once Justine Kalinsky tripped over him, causing his beloved Discman to crash to the ground, and he called her a dumb bitch. It would have been so easy to put him in his place, but I didn't say anything. Justine Kalinsky would have seen it as a declaration of friendship, and I'm not interested in putting in that much energy around here.

Thomas Mackee constantly burps loudly in class, and sometimes he tries to make a tune out of his burps. The song with the most requests is "Teenage Dirtbag," and it's actually fascinating to watch the level of appreciation for such a talent.

These guys fart a lot as well. I'm not saying that girls don't. We just aren't as passionate about them. The smell is sometimes overwhelming and I want to gag. They don't just limit these attacks to the classroom—they can come at you from anywhere around the school. The corridor, the stairwell, the canteen line. There's one area we call Fart Corridor because it belongs to the Year Eights and Nines, who are the biggest perpetrators. They make no apologies and feel no embarrassment. If a girl did one at St. Stella's she'd be an outcast for the rest of her natural life. Here, it's a badge of honor.

By term two, day two, period two, Tara Finke has had enough. She hands out slips to all thirty girls in the school and asks them to turn up for a lunchtime meeting where, quote, "The female proletariat are going to embark on the Revolution."

Oh, Tara.

No one turns up, of course. Tara Finke sees it as a success because Justine Kalinsky and I are there, and I want to point out to Tara that we haven't exactly "turned up." It's called having nowhere else to go. But Tara is in denial and she gets Justine Kalinsky to take the minutes. Justine makes a list of our names and then a list of all those absent, as if they've sent their apologies, and that takes up half our lunchtime.

"Suggestions?" Tara Finke asks.

"The most logical and persuasive one of us should go and see one of the House coordinators," Justine says, scribbling down a list of names under the heading "L and P," obviously for "logical and persuasive." "Someone who can argue our case with passion and sensitivity."

A Year Ten boy walks by and clutches his crotch.

"Don't these people realize that their bourgeois mentality is a manifestation of two thousand years of patriarchal crap?" Tara Finke snaps, giving him the finger.

I watch Justine discreetly cross Tara Finke's name off the "L and P" list.

We have a House meeting during period four. I'm in Kelly, which is named after a dead Brother who took in thirty boys off the streets of Sydney in the 1800s and then died of diphtheria.

The school doesn't have a school captain. It has six House leaders in Year Twelve, and ours is William Trombal. He's the shirt-rolled-up-to-his-elbow, no-nonsense type. He always has a frown on his face and looks slightly harassed and I think the girls-being-at-his-school thing doesn't impress him in the slightest. He's in charge of sports reports each week, and having to stand through such detail, spoken with such reverence, makes me want to yell, "It's just a ball game, for crying out loud."

My grandmother knows William Trombal's grandmother, which I think makes him half Italian. She claims that William Trombal's grandmother stole her S biscuit recipe and she dislikes her with a passion, although they pray together in the same Rosary group each week. Not that William Trombal and I have ever acknowledged this connection.

Tara Finke nudges me. "Fascism at its best here. They train them young."

I ignore her. My theory is to lay low, and my reluctance to get involved has nothing to do with fear or shyness, contrary to popular perception. I have this belief that people hate change and, more than anything, they hate those who try to change things. I might not be interested in being in the most popular group in the world, but I'm less interested in being an outcast. Anyway, my being political would make Mia happy and I wouldn't want that. She thinks she knows who I am because she thinks who I am is who *she* tells me I am.

"God they love the sound of their own voices," Tara Finke mutters.

And you don't?

Suddenly, I feel everyone's gaze on us. I look up and William Trombal is glaring, his dark eyes slicing straight through me.

"Do you have a question?" he asks, totally ignoring Tara and looking straight at me.

Tara Finke is scribbling something down on the lunchtime list of complaints. She passes it to me and I skim the list. At the bottom she's written, *Ask him where he got the pole up his ass from.*

The whole House is looking our way. I spot Luca, who gives me a sympathetic smile.

"We were just wondering . . . ," Tara Finke begins.

I can't believe she's going to make things worse. I look at the coat of arms behind William Trombal's head, which is full of Latin pretension.

". . . if the *P* stands for *pace* . . . peace . . . ," I finish off for her. I feel her glaring at me, but it is not as bad as the smug, condescending look on William Trombal's face.

"You're saying it in Italian," he says, like he's speaking to a moron. "In Latin it's *pax.*" Then he deliberately turns around to look at the coat of arms and then looks back at me. "And there's no *P* there, anyway. It's a *V*. For *veritas*. 'Truth.' " He pauses for emphasis after each word. "But I can understand how the *VIP* thing could confuse you."

"Ripped," Thomas Mackee behind me snickers, suggesting that William Trombal has well and truly won the point in this exchange.

When the meeting is over, Ms. Quinn, our House dean, is standing there in front of me. She holds out her hand and I realize I still have Tara's note.

"Can you come to my office?"

I sit in front of Ms. Quinn, watching as she reads the list. Most of the time she looks highly strung or half-bemused. She's pretty tough and doesn't give an inch, but I think that's how she has to be. My mother began her teaching career in a boys' school, and she said that every day was like going to war and every day she'd come home with battle fatigue. Ms. Quinn is youngish, but not teenage-boy lust material. I think they like her, but they still call her a bitch behind her back. She's spoken to me once or twice about some screw-ups on my timetable, but that's as far as it's ever gone.

"I like this," she says after a moment. I recognize the look in her eye. It's that Tara Finke/Mia Spinelli look. "I think you should have issues. This must be hard on you girls. I'll set you up with Will and he'll work through these requests with you."

I'm already picking up my bag. I'm not interested in dealing with William Trombal so soon after this morning's alphabet lesson.

"Tara Finke would probably prefer to do that," I say politely.

"According to this, Tara Finke thinks that Will has an object protruding from a part of his body," she explains to me politely. "I don't think she's the right person to speak to him."

"I don't think I am either."

She smiles and hands me back the list. "If he came across as gruff, it's because he's actually quite shy."

I nod. It's a blowing-her-off nod. It works, because she looks past me to the door as if to say, "You can go now." I do the polite-smile thing and, relieved, I turn around.

And walk straight into William Trombal.

We're almost exactly the same height, so eye contact is inevitable. I find a scar between his eyes to concentrate on. He has a strange face. It's all sharpness and angles and incredibly fair skin. But then he's got this thatch of black hair that's such a contrast.

It's like two cultures had a massive fight over his face and neither won.

"The girls are just having a few issues that they thought maybe you could iron out," Ms. Quinn explains.

"About?"

His voice is deep and gravelly. I once heard one of the girls say that he had the voice of a sex god, but because I've never really heard what a sex god sounds like, I can't verify that.

The list in my hand suddenly feels like a hot wedge against my palm. I don't want to hand it over. Apart from the comment about him, Tara Finke has this tampon machine obsession and she insisted on putting it at the top of the list. He holds out his hand, and I'm hating Tara Finke's guts for putting me through this.

He runs his eyes over the list, and I know the exact moment that he's reached the final line. His face flushes red and then he looks at me.

"What's your name?"

"Francis . . . Francesca . . . Spinelli."

Your grandmother stole my grandmother's S biscuit recipe, as you well know.

"I was going to be called Francesca," Ms. Quinn tells us. She nods, looking at us both. "But my mother went for Anna Carina."

I don't know how to react to this piece of trivia, so I smile politely.

"Were your parents Trotsky fans?" William Trombal asks, not at all perturbed by her rambling.

I wait for her to correct him but she doesn't. He might think he's the king of Latin translation, but he knows nothing about Russian literary history.

"Do you want some advice, Francis Francesca?" he asks me.

It's kind of one of those rhetorical things, because I can already tell he's going to give it to me.

He sighs and sits on the corner of the desk in an attempt to be as accessible as possible.

"Try to keep low-key. If you make a fuss, the guys aren't going to like it. There's going to be a shitload of stuff around here—sorry, Ms. Quinn—that you're not going to like, and being vocal about it will give you a rep you don't want."

I nod as if it's the best advice I've ever received. "I'll pass that on to the—"

Before I can finish, he turns away and sits down, his back to me, as if I was never there. I stare at the back of his head. There's something about it that makes me want to commit a violent act with a blunt instrument.

"It's Tolstoy, by the way," I say as I open the door.

He turns around. "What?"

Shut up, I tell myself. *Shut up.*

"The writer of *Anna Karenina.* Not Trotsky. Trotsky was a revolutionary who was stabbed with a pickax in Mexico in 1940. But I can understand how the *T* thing could confuse you."

He looks at me, his eyes narrowing. William Trombal doesn't like to be put in his place. Bad move.

I look at Ms. Quinn. She's smiling.

"Thank you, Ms. Quinn," I say politely, and walk out.

My father makes us an omelette for dinner. The three of us sit eating in silence. There has never, ever been silence at our dinner table, and tonight it's like torture.

"Should I take some in to Mummy?" Luca asks.

At home, at our most vulnerable, she's *Mummy*. When we're talking to other people she's *Mum,* but in my head she's just *Mia* because I've been angry at her so many times that I've wanted to distance myself from her. Everything Mia does has to be so out there and noticeable. She's the loudest of the daughters-in-law, was the most opinionated mother at St. Stella's, and more than once I saw my Stella friends roll their eyes at something she'd suggest we should do. We just wanted to have fun. Mia wanted us to change the world.

There's always a story to be told to show how weak I am and how great she is. "Remember the time you almost drowned?" she'd ask me. I don't want to remember. Because it's probably a reminder of how I needed saving.

"Mummy's eaten," my dad says.

"When?" I ask.

"Before you got home."

"That would have been lunch."

"Frankie, eat your food and be quiet!"

Luca and I exchange glances and look at my dad. Somehow he's becoming someone we don't know, as well.

I try to swallow the omelette, but it gets stuck in my throat. I want to go and throw it up, like my mum has for the past two mornings. I want to puke my guts out and I want her to come up behind me and hold back my hair and I want to take in her scent and I want to cry like I always do when I'm sick and my mum is there.

But I manage to swallow it, and the knowledge that it's sitting there in my stomach, like some kind of poison, makes me feel weak.

18

The place is beginning to look like a pigsty. My dad isn't the tidiest cook, and there are plates and frying pans all over the place. We clean up, but it doesn't look the same as when my mum gets us to do it.

Later, as I make my way to my room, I see Luca at her door. She calls him in and I can tell he feels uneasy about it. Their bedroom has always been our sanctuary. Sometimes at night we'll end up on their bed just talking. My dad will be snoring and Mia will say, "Turn around, Bobby, you're snoring," and he'll turn around and for a moment it'll be silent. Then he'll erupt into a massive snore and Luca and I will kill ourselves laughing and my dad will wake up and bark, "Get to bed!" and not even a second later he'll be snoring and we'll kill ourselves laughing again and Mia will say, "What is this? Grand Central Station?"

But their room isn't Grand Central Station anymore. It's a room my mum won't leave and I don't understand why and nobody will explain it to me, and later I find myself standing outside their door listening for anything.

And I hear nothing because it's like the volume button has been turned down on our lives and nobody has anything to say anymore.

chapter 3

IN RELIGION CLASS, we're put into pairs and given butcher's paper. It's a Catholic school thing, butcher's paper. Even butchers themselves have moved on to other alternatives. But ever since I can remember, it's played an important role in any decision-making process at school. Sometimes I wonder if the Pope gets out the butcher's paper over at the Vatican to explain the hierarchy of the church; or to draw a scaffold, listing potential leaders; or to illustrate how to get on with your fellow cardinals during a peer assessment session.

Today we're asked to come up with our ideal community, and I get stuck with Thomas Mackee, who scribbles something down on a piece of paper and hands it over to me. His ideal community has "no fat chicks, no rules, no one over twenty-five."

I look at the list and then at him and screw it up in a ball. Back at Stella's, my group were the queens of the butcher's paper presentation, and here I am stuck with a sexist, anarchist ageist. Fifteen minutes later we haven't written a thing, and Mr. Brolin reaches our desk and stares. He has a big us-and-them attitude about students, and I'm surprised he hasn't drawn a circle around his desk to keep us out of his area.

"You can't think of anything?" he asks.

"I gave her a list and she wasn't interested," Thomas Mackee says in a singsong voice.

"You can both stay after school and do it."

"Like I really want to *do it* with her," Thomas Mackee snickers when Mr. Brolin walks away.

The guys around us join in the snickering.

My ideal community?

Anywhere but here.

At 3:30, the butcher's paper is still in front of me. Mr. Brolin sits at the front calling his detention roll. There are a few kids from the junior school and a guy from my physics class. His name is Jimmy Hailler and he's in trouble for calling Brother Louis, our English teacher, Bro. He said, "Hey, Bro, how's it hanging?" Bro actually didn't mind it, but Mr. Brolin overheard and went ballistic.

Next to me, Thomas Mackee is doing his own thing, scribbling away. Whatever he's doing makes him grunt with frustration, but we've got an agreement. I come up with "our" ideal community and he stays out of my hair.

I watch Jimmy Hailler terrorize the kid next to him. Not that he's doing anything but speaking to him, but *that* is his form of terror. I've seen him do it to the introverted math geniuses in our year, who at times find themselves unable to escape his grasp.

"How are you, man?" he'll ask them, although he's never spoken a word to them all their lives.

They smile politely, wanting him to go away.

"Is that the new calculator you've got there?"

The questions are not threatening. The voice is not menacing. But one is suspicious, and relieved when he stops. He knows quite well that he's intimidating. The tapping on the desk with his pen, the tune he plays along to on his knee with his hand. He's like a time bomb waiting to explode and you don't want him anywhere near you.

Sometimes I think that Jimmy Hailler is a tool planted by teachers to stop students from getting into trouble. The juniors are more frightened by the prospect of having to sit next to him than anything else, and I'm sure troublemaking could be halved if they advertised the fact that he was on detention for the afternoon.

He catches me looking at him and gives me a grin. I'm unimpressed and he can sense it, and I stare down at the page in front of me.

My ideal community?

1. My mum is fine and can get out of bed.
2. St. Stella's goes to Year Twelve and I'm still with my friends.
3. No boy bands.
4. No Tara Finkes or Justine Kalinskys or Siobhan Sullivans.
5. Buffy slays teenage boys who burp and fart.
6. People on power trips are prohibited from being teachers.
7. Italy wins the World Cup (that one's for Luca).

I write it all down in my head, but not on the sheet in front of me. Because I don't want Thomas Mackee or Mr. Brolin to know anything about my ideal world. Because I know they'll do everything to mock it.

I scribble something down and lean back in my seat. Thomas

Mackee is listening to his Discman, as usual, and writing what looks like music notes, and it's driving him crazy, which is a pleasure to see.

I look at him.

"It's odious," he says.

"Detention?" I ask, confused.

"Huh?"

We have no idea what the other is talking about.

"What's odious?" I ask.

"O.D.S.," he says, pointing to his Discman and obviously referring to some loser band.

Like I really care.

Mr. Brolin walks down to us and looks at the sheet and then at me and Thomas Mackee. "Your ideal community has"—he squints his eyes, reading my writing—"no butcher's paper?"

Thomas Mackee looks at me as if I've lost it. Jimmy Hailler turns around and grins his little evil grin. Mr. Brolin gives us a week of detentions.

I've turned into a delinquent.

My father looks at my school diary when I get home. I have to get it signed and show it to Mr. Brolin. School diaries have always been Mia's area.

We're down in the laundry room trying to find Luca's spare school shirt.

"Don't start getting into trouble, Frankie. Not now," he says, looking through the laundry basket.

"I hate this school. I want to go to Pius."

"That's not possible."

"Why? It's not too late."

"Mia wants you at St. Sebastian's."

"It's ruining my life."

He finds the shirt.

"Do you know how to use the washing machine?"

"Papa, are you listening to me?"

He bangs on the back window and I can see Luca playing soccer outside with some neighborhood kids.

"Homework," he shouts.

Luca pretends he can't hear. He's too busy being Mark Viduka, scoring a goal and then dropping to his knees and holding his hands up. Luca takes after Mia. He's very dramatic and emotional.

My father starts the washing machine, and after a moment it begins making its way toward us like something out of a sci-fi film.

I watch my father trying to deal with the possessed washing machine. We have no idea what to do because one part of Mia's doctrine is to teach us independence while the other is to keep us dependent on her. It drives me crazy, because it's such a fantastic ploy—she can complain and make us look like the bad guys while she's the martyr.

I decide I'm going to tell Mia what I think. That what she's doing is selfish and it's ruining all our lives and that I'm going to go to Pius with my Stella friends because she can't go around making decisions about my life, removing me from my security blankets and then leaving me hanging on my own.

I go upstairs and stand in Mia's doorway. That's where most of our conversations tend to take place these days.

"I'm going to wash the clothes," I tell her.

"I'll do it." She tries to sit up.

You said that yesterday, I want to yell at her.

"Come in here and sit with me."

"I can't. Luca doesn't have any school shirts and Daddy doesn't know how to use the washing machine."

I step into the room anyway. It smells unhealthy. Not like the sandalwood and rosemary scents I'm used to. I get closer to the bed and she smiles weakly. Her skin, usually rich and smooth, looks pasty. Her dark eyes are huge and bloodshot, and she looks kind of old. Not the Mia who thinks it's a crime to leave the house without lipstick and who still has guys perving at her although she's forty.

I edge to the side of the bed and she sits up.

"Don't fight with Daddy," she tells me tiredly.

I nod. I want to crawl into bed next to her but I'm scared I won't want to get out.

"I'm going to try to be better tomorrow. I promise," she says.

Her voice is pitiful. Who is this person? I can't help thinking how strange her words are. Does it mean she has control over this thing, whatever it is?

"I've got a week's detention," I tell her miserably.

"What did you do?"

"I made a protest about butcher's paper."

She tries to make a joke. "I knew I brought you up well."

She can hardly speak. It's as if she has absolutely no energy and I'm tiring her out.

Later, my father gives up on Luca and homework, and I can't be bothered doing mine either. We watch television until 11:30 and eat all the junk food in the cupboard. I could feel guilty about taking advantage of the situation, but I can't be bothered. I can't be bothered about anything. Later, in bed, I put my Discman in my ear and, like every night of my life, I let the music put me to sleep.

Left alone with a dial tone . . . excuse me, operator, why is no one listening?

Chapter 4

ON SATURDAY NIGHT, I meet up with the ex–Stella girls. We try to do this as often as possible, so when I rang them during the week they invited me to a party at Maroubra, which is out in the eastern suburbs, near the beach.

"Everyone will be there," Michaela said.

At Pius, the ex–Stella girls have got into the swing of things easily. They seem to know everyone at the party, and it all seems so effortless to them, as if they've known these people all their lives. But they've always been good at fitting in and getting on with as many people as possible. At Stella's, the teachers and other girls loved them, while I seemed to make enemies without even trying. I was either talking too much in Year Seven, or not talking enough in Year Eight. I was too smart for my own good, or not working to my potential. One year they'd tell me that I needed to be put in my place, the next year I'd be told to find a place of my own, rather than letting the girls find it for me.

When my dad drops me off, they scream hysterically.

"Look at your hair," they say. I'm confused, because my hair looks exactly the same as it has for the last five years. Shoulder-length, brown, straight.

I see familiar faces from Stella's inside the house, and they wave from a distance.

"So, who are you hanging out with?" Natalia asks as we sit on the front veranda, while guys hang around, perving. These guys are different from those at Sebastian's. They are actually more interested in us than each other.

"Siobhan Sullivan and Justine Kalinsky?" Michaela teases, and they all groan.

I force a smile and laugh. "The Perpetua girls are really cool," I say, not exactly lying.

"Who are the other girls?" a Pius hanger-on asks.

"Siobhan Sullivan is the biggest slut in the whole wide world," Teresa, the Queen of Hyperbole, tells them. "Francis used to hang out with her in Year Seven."

They call me Francis, by the way. "Just to keep you simple," they'd tell me.

"I swear to God, this girl never shut up before we met her. Even the teachers would say, 'Francis, enough of these questions.'"

"Once in Year Seven on an excursion to Manly, we were on the ferry coming back and next minute she's on the bow of the boat screaming out, 'I'm the Queen of the World,'" Simone says.

"And remember, we thought, what a psycho?" Natalia says, as usual ending all her sentences up in the air. "And you got suspended, Francis? And the school wanted you tested for ADHD and your mum went berserk?"

Faintly.

"And then Siobhan Sullivan went away for a couple of weeks and we thought, let's make friends with her, because I think this girl needs saving."

When Siobhan Sullivan's grandfather died in Year Seven, she went up north to stay with her nan. They were the loneliest days of my life. Not one person would let me hang out with them. "It's because you're a show-off," my future friends explained to me gently. "If you stop showing off, we'll be your friends."

"And we made her ours," Michaela says, hugging me to her affectionately.

That's what my friends do. They're press agents. They give me publicity, and for three months at Sebastian's I haven't had any, so it's a bit of a relief to be on the news again.

"And the other girl?"

"Justine Kalinsky, *poor thing*. She came new in Year Eight. Do you remember in Year Eight?" Natalia asks the others.

"Oh my God, Year Eight. Yeah," Michaela says.

"This one time in Year Eight we had to write on butcher's paper how we'd like people to see us. Remember ours? We were like, 'We don't want people to see us as leaders or heroes or anything out of the ordinary. We just want them to see us as on their level.'"

"But Justine Kalinsky gets up there, on her own, *poor thing*. And she says, 'I'd like people to see me as their Rock.'"

"And we killed ourselves laughing."

"Poor thing."

"What did she mean?" the Pius girl asks.

"Who knows."

I don't dare mention Tara Finke. Sluts and losers are tolerable to my friends. But a person with a social conscience is from Pluto. Once in Year Nine, Mia forced me to go to the Palm Sunday peace march and I had to walk alongside Tara Finke. Our photo got into the school news, and I didn't hear the end of it for ages.

A group of girls walk up the garden path and my friends scream and join them, leaving me with the Pius hanger-on, who confides that if it weren't for my friends, she'd be lost.

"They saved me from having to hang out with the losers," she tells me with pride.

"That's what they do," I explain politely.

We smile at each other with nothing left to say.

It's a good night.

When I see Justine Kalinsky at school, I feel guilty, as if I've spent the whole weekend bitching about her.

"Tara's talking to them about a basketball game." Justine Kalinsky is giggling with excitement.

I sit at my desk, listening to Eva Rodriguez and the rest of the Perpetua girls being persuaded by Tara Finke.

"It's the best idea ever," Justine Kalinsky says, beaming.

"Can you arrange it?" Eva Rodriguez asks.

It takes a moment to realize that they're talking to me.

"Me?"

"Justine reckons you've already set up communication with one of the House leaders."

Justine Kalinsky's face is lit up in anticipation.

"Which one?" one of the other Perpetua girls asks.

"Trombal," Tara Finke says.

The girls are impressed.

"I don't think he actually likes dealing with her," Tara Finke says. "But if we send someone new, he'll interpret it as a lack of leadership on our part. Let's be consistent."

"Plus we can't send someone with a strong personality because the guys will get defensive. She's perfect," Siobhan Sullivan says. She's enthusiastic about something for once, probably because it means getting into Lycra in front of a bunch of boys.

"It's not competitive. Just call it a friendly senior basketball game. It'll give us some kind of profile."

"They'll slaughter us," one of the other girls argues.

"I play rep," Eva Rodriguez tells us. "Plus our school won the Eastern Region last year and five of us from that team are here."

"Ours got to the finals in the Inner-Western," Justine Kalinsky pipes up. "Not that I was on the team, but Francesca was."

"I think it's a great idea," Tara Finke says. "This is our foot in the door, and we should grab the opportunity and show them that we have the ability to take control of our lives at this school."

They all look at me.

How can my weak personality resist such a challenge?

William Trombal and the other leaders have a little office just outside Administration.

I stand out front for a moment or two and hear music coming from inside. I knock on the door and walk in. He's in there

31

with another two House leaders, and they all look up for a moment.

"Yours?" one of the House leaders asks him, smirking at me. I look away for a moment, concentrating on the poster of two league stars with bloodstained faces hugging each other.

"I'll see you later," I hear Trombal tell the other guys as they walk past me out the door.

When we're alone, he sits back in his chair and turns down the music.

"I'm not going to get into a discussion about a tampon machine," he tells me bluntly.

I don't respond, and he looks at me and holds up one hand as if to say, *What?*

So much for Ms. Quinn's "he's actually quite shy."

"The girls would like to arrange a game with the guys."

"We don't play netball."

"Basketball."

He gives a laugh, but he's not laughing with me.

"I don't want to sound patronizing, but we won the CBSA finals last term."

"Just a goodwill game," I explain.

"We wouldn't want to hurt you," he says. "The guys can be aggressive."

"Tell them it's friendly."

He thinks for a moment, looking me straight in the eye.

Don't look away, I tell myself. But then I regret not looking away, because I feel my face going red and I don't know why.

"Who's your captain?" he asks.

32

"Eva Rodriguez."

"Good-looking girl who looks like Jennifer Lopez?"

I'm poker-face cool and it's killing me, but I don't say anything. He fishes something out of his pocket and I notice that it's our list of requests, and I can't help being surprised that he has it on him. He opens it up and reads down the list, and for a moment I see the paper flap, as if the hand holding it can't control itself, and then I realize that William Trombal is nervous.

I'm making him nervous.

"Request number four," he says, reading from the list. "An opportunity to play competitive sports."

I nod, as if I know exactly what request number four is.

"Why not?" he says with a shrug.

I hold out my hand to shake on it. Luca and I do that all the time, and for a moment I feel so childish, but I'm too embarrassed to retrieve the hand.

"No complaining if anyone breaks a nail?" he asks, looking at my outstretched hand, but he doesn't extend his.

"You can complain all you like. You can cry as well," I tell him.

I get a hint of a smile and then he shakes my hand.

"I'll see what the guys say."

"Thank you."

"What did you say your name was? Francis . . ."

"My name's Francesca."

Detention drags on. Thomas Mackee sits next to me, scribbling on what looks like a music sheet. He's a guitarist. Sometimes, as he's walking to music class, he serenades Ms. Quinn, who, despite his being an idiot, actually has a bit of a giggle. He nudges me, almost sending me sprawling.

"Do you know how to convert notes into tablature?" he asks me in his duh-brain voice.

I pretend he's not there.

"Are you retarded?" he asks.

I ignore him.

"Do you know anything?"

This coming from the Big Kahuna of Knowledge.

"Do you?" he presses.

"I know you're a dickhead, and for the time being, that's all I need to know," I say flatly.

"Ooh, you're turning me on."

That's as clever as our conversations get. Sometimes Jimmy Hailler joins in when he's not torturing the younger kids. Thomas Mackee and Jimmy Hailler grasp each other's hands, one of those brothers-in-arms-we-fought-in-Nam-together grips, but outside this room I don't think they relate.

"What's the punishment today?" Jimmy Hailler asks.

"Ten different lines. Must have some form of the word 'learn' in it," Thomas Mackee tells him. He adopts the voice of a deep and meaningful television psychologist, matching his words to hand actions. "He wants us to take control of our misbehavior so we can self-discipline ourselves."

Jimmy Hailler looks over my shoulder and reads what I've written.

I must not underestimate the wisdom of my learned teachers.

Butcher's paper is not just for wrapping sausages, but for learning."

"That was mine," Thomas Mackee says. He's very proud.

Jimmy Hailler looks at me and I nod in confirmation.

"Wow."

"*Learn Baby Learn, Disco Inferno.*"

"Hers," Thomas Mackee says. "Have no idea what it means."

"*I came, I mucked around, thus I did not learn.*"

When we're allowed to go, I leave as quickly as possible. Through Hyde Park, I walk ahead of them, hoping that they don't speak to me. On the bus, Thomas Mackee and I sit at opposite ends. I'm grateful that he doesn't see solidarity in our detention. I figure he lives somewhere around Stanmore, because he gets off the stop before mine.

At Stella's, we all came from the same area, and I liked the closeness of it all. Here, I don't feel a sense of community. The city is too big and the school is like an island at the edge of it. An island full of kids from all over Sydney, rather than from one suburb. Nothing binds it together; no one culture, no one social group. You could be on the same bus or train line with someone and still live miles apart. My bus line travels along Parramatta Road from the inner city, past the University of Technology, where Mia works, past the University of Sydney, and then into the beginning of the inner west. Most of the time I don't travel with Luca because he has choir practice or soccer or I have a three-unit class after school. At Stella's, our bus was a School Special and the trip home was the best part of the day. Here, it's almost the worst.

I get off at my usual stop on Parramatta Road and walk down Johnston Street. Sometimes Annandale feels like a small country town, ten minutes from downtown. There's still a working-class quality to it, but, sprinkled with academics, musicians, and professionals, it

35

tends not to have a "type," which suits Mia, who goes on about "types" all the time.

Once in a while, my parents toss up whether or not to move. My dad thinks that not providing us with space will stunt our emotional growth and that it's cruel to have a dog and children when you've got a tiny backyard. But we're not interested in that type of space, and neither is our dog. He loves having his puppaccinos at Cafe Bones over in Leichhardt every Saturday morning or sitting outside Bar Italia while we have gelato and coffee. Luca named him because Mia's into that. I got to name Luca, so he got to name the dog, and I thank God he's younger than I am, because the dog's name is Pinocchio. I named Luca after a character in a Suzanne Vega song. I didn't realize until I was older that the person in the song gets abused. I just loved the certainty the character had about who he was.

Luca's one of those blessed kids. Incredibly cute, smart, and has the voice of an angel, which is why he's in a composite class of Year Five and Six for choir kids at St. Sebastian's. William Trombal used to be a choirboy as well, but these days his role is merely to take the choirboys over for morning practice. According to Luca, he lets them play cricket in the middle aisle of the cathedral with a hacky sack. Apparently, the hacky sack once hit Christ on the cross, and William Trombal said that if Christ's hands weren't nailed on to that cross, he would have caught the ball himself.

Luca says that when he grows up, he wants to be just like William Trombal. Fantastic. My little brother's ambition is to be a stick-in-the-mud moron with no personality.

I have absolutely no idea what I want to be when I grow up. I've changed my mind one hundred times. Just once I'd like to get it all together, see beyond the next five minutes, but I've never been able to. Not even when I was a kid. Mia's mother, Nonna Celia, is to blame for that, because she's a prophet of doom. Every time I'd ask her if we could go someplace the next day or next week, her reply would be, "We might not live that long." If I'd say, "See you tomorrow," her answer would be, "If that's what God wants." Leaving so much to fate has kept me an insomniac for most of my life, and this thing with Mia has reinforced the fear.

I get to the house, trying my hardest to avoid the people across the road. As usual, I wonder why they even have a house. They spend all their free time sitting on the front veranda watching the world go by. They eat outside with their meals on their lap trays, hang over the fence on either side for chats, while their children, grandchildren, and any other kids they seem to be looking after play happily on the little stretch of grass in front of their house. I don't know how many live there because they always seem to have people over, but it's like four generations in one tiny pre-fab house, like something out of a 1940s *Harp in the South* story. Although they're doing nothing wrong, everything about them annoys me. So when they wave, I never wave back.

I've heard Mia talk to them about me. "She's going through that adolescent alien stage," she told them once. "Where she has to pretend she's something she's not."

As opposed to being who *she* thinks I am, or should be. Maybe another Tara Finke. That'd make me popular.

Today I want them to wave, just to reassure me that everything is normal. But their happiness makes me angry. So I just go inside, praying that Mia is marking assignments, or cooking dinner, or on the phone counseling her friend Freya, the "bastard magnet," or gossiping with Zia Teresa, or arguing with my dad, or kissing my dad, or reading, or laughing with my cousin Angelina, or sneaking a look at *The Bold and the Beautiful*.

But God's not listening.

It's been six days.

The door's still closed.

Chapter 5

THE BASKETBALL GAME draws a lunchtime crowd in the gym. Not just the basketballers, but most of the girls and half of the guys. The boys' team is made up of Year Eleven and Twelve boys, and I notice that William Trombal is one of them, but thankfully not Thomas Mackee, who is too busy eating a meat pie illegally in the back row. Once in a while he gives a war cry and meat pie goes everywhere.

Ms. Quinn sits at the front, chatting to one of the other teachers. She looks pleased. Even Brother Edmund, the principal, makes an appearance, and I watch him shake hands with William Trombal.

The guys huddle together and do a Sebastian's chant.

Glory, glory, alleluia,
Sebastian boys are going to rule ya.
We'll beat you in the end
And we'll perfect it as a trend.
And you'll go home black-and-blue.

A real Wordsworth, the one who made that up!

The girls stand around pretending to warm up. We've never been a team before. We don't have a chant and we've barely spoken in front of these boys, let alone sung. A warning bell is rung by Justine Kalinsky, who is in her element, because she has a role to play for once in this school. I look around and see Luca, who holds up a hand. I give him a smile, and the whistle blows and a cheer goes up.

This feeling comes over me. A positive one for once. A sense of accomplishment and, I hate to say it, pride. The girls are happy, the guys are accommodating, and for a moment I get a feeling that everything's going to be just fine.

I am a success at last.

We get annihilated. There is no mercy. The word "friendly" is never used in the same context again. "Friendly," according to *The Australian Little Oxford Dictionary*, means "acting or disposed to act as friend." The word "act" is very apt. The girls glare at me. They need to put a face to their misery and I'm it. From then on, whenever someone uses the words "the basketball game," there is no question which one they are referring to.

This is the short version: They play like it's the Olympics and their country's honor depends on it. If we even dare to try to adjust our gym pants, we get wolf-whistled. There are nosebleeds, fractured fingers, and hair pulling. It's pretty full-on, and although I'm tall, I feel as if I've been tossed around the whole game. I end up on my bum so many times that I'm convinced I've broken a bone there.

At one point, I end up underneath a heap of bodies in a last-minute rumble, clutching the ball to my stomach, not wanting to let go of it for all the money in the world. It's there, in that dark huddle of sweat and testosterone and hot breath and heaving breasts and erections, that I get the clearest of pictures. Because somehow I find myself straddled by William Trombal and I see the gleam of something in his face as he pulls the ball out of my hands. Not lust. Not adrenaline. It's something much more sinister. It's revenge, and I begin to understand the truth. That it all would have turned out very differently if Trotsky had written *Anna Karenina*.

Later, I sit in the gym alone. Not exactly pondering the game, because it's not worth it. Just having my own time-out; a bit of self-pity here, a bit of self-loathing there. There are few places in this school to take a breather without the whole world watching.

William Trombal walks in to collect some of the sports gear. He's cheerful, for once, whistling to himself. When he grabs the stuff, he walks over, knowing he can't ignore me.

"Good game," he says. "We should do it again sometime."

I look at him and don't answer. There are no comebacks. What am I going to say? "Yes, it was a great game. Put me through it again. Anytime you want." So silence is my only weapon.

"Hope there's no hard feelings because of the winning margin."

"Can I have our list back?" I ask.

"List?"

"The one with all our requests. Tampons? Girls' sports? Respect? That list."

"You're taking this personally, I can tell."

"And you didn't?"

I pick up my bag and begin to walk away.

"What's that supposed to mean?" he asks.

"Great talking to you. We should do it again sometime," I say without turning back.

My dad takes Luca and me to Bar Italia in Leichhardt. We almost get Mia out the door, but by the time we're leaving, she's already gone back to her bedroom, leaving the three of us with no desire for anything. We go anyway, pretending that it's no big deal. Pretending that it's normal for my dad, Luca, and me to go for gelato on our own. But it's not normal. Nothing about our lives, at the moment, is normal.

It's difficult sitting there without people you know coming up to say "Hi!" every once in a while.

"How's Mia?" they ask good-naturedly. "You guys keeping her busy as usual?"

The three of us have smiles plastered on our faces as we nod with enthusiasm.

"You know Mia," Dad jokes, "if she's not doing a hundred things at once she's not happy."

We feel like criminals. Liars. When we get a moment to ourselves, we try to speak about it.

"Is she getting better?" Luca asks.

"It's not that easy," Dad says.

"Is it because she does everything?" I ask.

"No."

"Is it our—"

"No," he says harshly. "No," he repeats gently. "Everything's going to be fine. She'll be back at work soon. Let's just keep the house clean."

Oh yeah, I want to say, *because a clean house will result in peace in the Middle East as well.*

Later, my cousin Angelina comes over. She's shrewd, and I get an inkling that the family has been talking about what's happening with my mum and has sent her over on some kind of surveillance mission. Relatives sometimes call Angelina mini-Mia because they have the same fiery personality, although my mum's her aunt by marriage only. Despite the ten-year difference, they get on fantastically. They're brutally honest and don't take shit from anyone. Angelina's getting married later this year. Angus, her fiancé, is probably one of the most uncomplicated guys I've ever come across, a bit like my dad. Her brothers used to say they'd pity the guy she'd end up with because he'd need to be a saint, but that's because my cousins think they know everything and have their wives convinced of that as well. It's incredible to witness how clueless they actually are.

Angelina's in with my mum for ages and I want it to be like the days when Angelina, Mia, and I would have our secret women's business coffees. I've never been left out of their conversations, not even when they talk about sex (although when my mum talks about her sex life with my dad, I feel like being sick). Tonight, I'm excluded and I try to piece things together from a distance, but I haven't got enough to go on.

When Angelina comes out, she kisses my cheek.

"Ring me about the bridesmaid dresses," she says, referring to her upcoming wedding and my role in it.

"What did you talk about?"

"I'll tell you about this later, Frankie. I promise you."

"Why not now, Angelina? My dad keeps on telling the University she's got the flu, but she hasn't."

She looks at me but doesn't speak for a moment, which is rare for Angelina.

"It's a bit of a breakdown. She just needs time out, you know?"

43

I shake my head. A bit down. A bit of a breakdown. A bit of bullshit. There are no "bits" to this. There are large chunks. Of information that everyone is keeping from Luca and me.

Angelina speaks to my dad outside for a while. Neighborhood Watch, across the road, are out there, of course, and I sit at the window watching them. How dare they be so happy. I block them out and decide to ring up Michaela from Stella's because if anyone's going to be there for me, she will be. Her mother answers the phone.

"It's Francesca."

"Who?"

"Francesca. Francesca Spinelli."

There is a silence and I realize that she doesn't know who I am even though I was at school with her daughter for four years.

"From Stella's," I mumble.

"Oh. How are you? Michaela's not here. She's out with her friends."

I thank her and hang up the phone and I feel like crap. I don't remember the last time anyone used my name, except for Ms. Quinn. I don't remember the last time anyone looked me in the eye to speak to me. I'm frightened to look at myself in the mirror because maybe nothing's there.

I miss the Stella girls telling me what I am. That I'm sweet and placid and accommodating and loyal and nonthreatening and good to have around. And Mia. I want her to say, "Frankie, you're silly, you're lazy, you're talented, you're passionate, you're restrained, you're blossoming, you're contrary."

I want to be an adjective again.

But I'm a noun.

A nothing. A nobody. A no one.

Chapter 6

LUCA AND I are late again and, as usual, we have to face William Trombal. Yet another role of the House leaders is to stand in the foyer and record the names of those in their House who are late. From the look on William Trombal's face each morning, I can tell it's his least favorite job.

He asks me my name for the fourth time this week. He knows I know he knows it, but he insists on this charade.

"Katarina Esperante," I tell him.

Luca looks from me to him and then back again as if I've gone insane.

William Trombal glances up from the late book in his hands. "That's not your name."

I don't answer and he looks at Luca and rolls his eyes.

"Luca Spinelli," Luca says politely, "and she's . . ."

I give him the Spinelli death stare.

". . . she's my sister."

William Trombal gives in and writes in my name. "You've been late four times this week," he says, stating the obvious.

I can sense Luca smiling politely next to me. He wants everyone to be happy and hates any kind of conflict. I pull him away and we walk down the stairs that lead to the quadrangle.

"You're not to talk to that guy," I tell him.

"He looks after Year Five, *Katarina*."

"What does that make him? God?"

He rolls his eyes. I pinch him and he pinches me back. That's how we do the affection thing in public.

For the rest of the day, I feel out of it. Not that I've ever felt into it around here. It's like I lose track of time. One minute I'm in English and when I next open my eyes I'm in legal studies, but I don't remember how I got there. On the page in front of me I've written stuff down, but I can't remember holding the pen. I want to rest my head on the desk and just sleep, and for most of the day I kind of do. I can tell the teachers don't like me. I remember the way they used to look at the apathetic girls at St. Stella's. I think teachers can even handle the troublemakers, but they hate the slackers and that's how they see me.

"Just ask me how I'm feeling," I want to say. "Just ask and I may tell you."

But no one does.

At lunchtime, I feel Justine Kalinsky watching me and when I look at her, she smiles, and I walk away and hide out in the toilets. Not the greatest place to spend forty minutes, but I just can't deal with Tara Finke and Justine Kalinsky today. I just want to

46

have a rest from all of that. I just want to lie down and not get up.

After ten minutes, I've had enough and I walk out of the toilets and across the courtyard and am beckoned over by the group who sit against the wall. These guys are European, and I know it's time to do the cultural-bond thing. Sometimes they nod at me. A you-and-me-are-the-same nod. I wonder if they ever nod at William Trombal.

"You Italian?" they ask.

I nod.

They pat the space next to them and I make myself comfortable.

"Portuguese," I'm told by the guy who called me over. His name is Javier, pronounced "Havier," and every time one of the teachers pronounces his name with a *J* in class, there's a booing sound.

"She's Italian," Javier tells one of the guys who joins them from the canteen.

"Third in the World Cup ranking," the guy says.

"Behind Brazil," another pipes up

"What's your team?" Javier asks.

It's a soccer thing. I think of Luca's bedroom. "Inter Milan."

Approval. Good choice.

The others are Diego, Tiago, and Travis, who they call a wannabe wog.

"You shy, Francesca?" Javier asks me later on.

I shake my head. "Not really." I'm just sad, I want to say. And I'm lonely.

When Javier speaks, he uses his middle fingers to point down, as if he's singing some hip-hop song. It's like the spirit of some rap singer has taken over his body.

"I like you, Francesca. I like the way you treat your brother. Like he's your friend, and that's why I'm telling you this. Guys don't like chicks who are down all the time."

I thank him for the advice. I'll make a point of telling my mum that tonight. I'll say, "Mum, guys don't go for sad chicks and you're making me incredibly sad and because of that you're curtailing my social life, so could you please get out of bed."

And then she'll get out of bed and we'll live happily ever after.

They call out to a guy on the basketball courts. I recognize him from my biology class. He's got a massive smile with big white teeth.

"Shaheen, what's happening?" Javier asks him.

"Did you see that shot? Did ya? Huh?" Shaheen asks.

"You're a legend, Shaheen."

"Lebs rule!"

Shaheen says that about five times a day.

"Where, mate? Where do the Lebs rule? How are they doing in soccer? Did they rule in the Olympics? How about tennis? Where's the Davis Cup team from Lebanon, Shaheen? Lobbing a few balls in Beirut?"

The bantering is good-natured.

"What do you reckon, Francesca?" Javier asks me. "Do Lebs rule?"

I look at Shaheen, who's grinning. I can't help grinning back. "My school captain last year was a Leb. So I guess she ruled."

Shaheen shakes my hand.

Suddenly I'm a girl with attitude.

Attitude is everything with these guys. I have no chance of being their goddess because Eva Rodriguez is. She's upbeat and positive. But somehow I'm allowed to be part of them, based purely on the

18

fact that my grandparents and theirs belong to a minority. I'm back in complacency land and I'm loving it.

They give me advice. Keep away from the SAS, they tell me. They're the guys who sit on the quadrangle stairs who have an obsession with the military. On non-uniform days they come to school wearing camouflage.

The bell rings and Shaheen walks me up to class and we sit together and he gives me a rundown on his hero, Tupac.

"He's not really dead," he tells me.

I have no idea who he's talking about, but I find the whole conspiracy theory surrounding a supposedly dead rapper more intriguing than biology.

And somehow, yet again, I've managed to get through another day.

My dad arrives home and goes straight to their room to see how she is. At the moment, my dad can only be Mia's husband, not Francesca and Luca's father.

Luca looks at me. "Do you think Mummy speaks to Papa at night?"

I don't know what to say to him.

"Because it's okay if she can't speak to us, but Papa would be so sad if she didn't speak to him."

"It's not as if she doesn't want to speak to us," I explain.

"It's just that Papa likes speaking to Mummy," he says, almost in tears. "He always wants to speak to her. Sometimes more than he wants to speak to us, so if she doesn't speak to him . . ."

Being Mia's husband has always been my dad's priority, even at the best of times, so now I feel as if we're orphans.

"Do you want to do your homework on my bed?" I ask.

He nods. I know he'll fall asleep there and I let him.

Later, I lie down next to him while he sleeps with Pinocchio snug up against him. Squashed up on the end of the bed, I try to think back to the day before my mum didn't get out of bed. What was the last thing she said to us? What clues did she leave that we didn't respond to? We own all this, and while we're owning this ugly sickness that turns off the lights in a person's head, those around us who think they know us best observe and comment.

I start wondering how the rest of the world sees us, and this is what I'm sure of.

They look at us as if we're guilty. My dad, Luca, and I have become the villains. I know what they're thinking. How could someone as lively and passionate as Mia feel this way? It's her family, they whisper in my head. They've sucked the life out of her. All three of them. They see my father for who he is out there in the real world and not the person he is in our home. They see him as the guy who rode around on my Malvern Star bike once and broke his arm, or the husband at Mia's university dinner parties who doesn't say much. They don't know the real him. Mia might be responsible for daily discipline, but if she wants to scare us, it's my dad who's in charge. That he doesn't believe in small talk and won't say much is because he's bored by people who talk crap. He can make Mia laugh when she's in the most stressed of moods. He can fix anything that's broken in our house and can pull apart a car engine and put it back together again and make it work. That's what people don't see, and the fact that he doesn't care what they think calms me down at the worst of times.

Then I picture the way they see me. *Have you seen the eldest?* I can hear them ask. *She's a dead loss. Has no idea what she wants to do with her life. She's so insipid, she's almost invisible. Her closest friend's mother didn't even know who she was.*

What about the son? He still sleeps with his sister and he's ten years old. No wonder Mia's given up.

I do the deals-with-God thing. *Make her better . . . make us all better and I'll change the world for you.*

But God doesn't talk to me. It's because every night I lie here with music in my ears and I say my prayers and fall asleep in the middle of them. He only talks to people like Mia. People he thinks are worth it. Because they have passion. They have something. I have nothing. I'm . . . *Keep awake, Francesca. Keep awake and start to pray.*

I'm a waste of space.

I am . . .

I . . .

My dad does the only thing he knows how to do this morning. He makes us eggs for breakfast.

"We don't like eggs, Papa," I finally tell him, because I think deep down I'm a bit pissed-off with him. Why can't he fix things up? "We never have."

He looks from Luca to me and then hurls the eggs against the stainless steel.

I watch the design they make as they run down the splashboard, and then he's crying. My dad is *crying* and Luca is hugging him from behind, saying, "I'll eat the eggs, Daddy, I'll eat the eggs," and he's

51

crying too and I can't bear watching them. All I want to do is scream out "What's happening?" over and over again because ten days ago my mum didn't get out of bed. No visible symptoms, no medicine, no doctors. My dad says she's a *bit down* and my cousin says it's a *bit of a breakdown.* I've looked up the word "breakdown" because I am desperate for any clue: "collapse, failure of health or power, analysis of cost." None of the definitions make sense to me. A breakdown of what, I'm not sure. But she doesn't eat, that I know.

It has almost become an obsession. Every morning I study the fridge and pantry to see what's there, and every afternoon I study them again to see if something's missing. But nothing is. There are no plates in the sink, no food wrappers in the garbage. No evidence of papers being marked or of the phone being answered. Nothing. *Nothing* makes sense. My mother won't get out of bed, and it's not that I don't know who she is anymore.

It's that I don't know who I am.

I stand in front of William Trombal for the fifth time this week. Luca tries to avoid his eyes. I don't know what we look like to him, but he doesn't ask our names. He just looks at us and for a moment I see sympathy, and I hate him for it.

No sermons today.

Even the prince of punishment doesn't think we're worth talking to.

Chapter 7

TODAY THE GRANDMOTHERS step in. Mia's been in bed for two weeks, and decisions about us are made. Luca goes to Zia Teresa's and I go to Nonna Anna's, and Nonna Celia moves into our house. Before I leave, I hear Nonna Celia and my dad talking. Nonna Celia wants to take Mia to her own doctor, but my dad says no. He always goes on about how Nonna Celia's doctor hands out prescription drugs to avoid dealing with the real issues. My dad tells her that everything's going to be okay, and it comforts me to hear that reassurance.

Luca sits on my bed as I pack away a few of my things. He looks just like a stereotypical little soccer freak, ball in his hand and the Inter Milan jersey dwarfing his skinny frame.

"What's happening?" he asks in a voice that doesn't sound like his anymore.

"Everything's going to be fine. You always have fun at Zia Teresa's."

What I hate about this most is that no one gets how we're feeling.

No one asks us if we want to be separated. They just presume that Luca will want to be with his cousins and I'll want peace and quiet.

He lies down next to me and we hold on to each other tight. I can't tell horror brother-and-sister stories about Luca and me. We're crazy about each other, and our arguments are limited to who gets control of the TV remote between 7:00 and 7:30 p.m.

Life at my grandparents' is a different story. Nonna Anna and Nonno Salvo are television fanatics, especially the game shows. If it's not *Wheel of Fortune,* it's *The New Price Is Right* or *Sale of the Century.* They have absolutely no idea what the questions asked are, but they are excited by the process and the colored lights and the money symbols flashing up at different intervals.

Then there's the news. The 5:00 p.m. news on Channel Ten (a difficult time for them because it clashes with *The New Price Is Right*), the 6:00 p.m. news on Channel Nine, the 7:00 p.m. national news, the Italian news on the Italian radio station, and if I stay awake long enough I get to watch the 10:30 p.m. *Lateline* on Public Broadcasting. It's a very frustrating process because they get most of it wrong. Nonno Salvo calls out obscenities at the man whose image appears behind the newscaster's head as she tells us the top story of the night. Nonno explains to me that the bastard pictured is a war criminal who is responsible for the deaths of a village of men in Bosnia. In actual fact, it's Rupert Murdoch, but I don't try to explain.

Tonight, we watch a cop show where someone gets shot dead. Nonno Salvo reassures me that the person's not really dead. It's just an actor. Then my nonna tells him that of course I know that.

"She has the mouth of a viper," he tells me, twisting his bottom lip with his finger to further illustrate the point.

Ever since I can remember, my nonno and nonna have had these arguments. This one lasts a whole twenty-two minutes. It has to end because *Who Wants to Be a Millionaire* is just about to start and no talking is allowed during that. But I suppose they love each other to death. Every year at my nonna's annual surprise birthday party, where she pretends she has no idea that we're all huddled inside her kitchen, although the fifteen cars parked outside would be a certain giveaway, we go berserk when photos are taken and Nonno tries to kiss her and she acts coy. When he gets to lock lips for more than ten seconds, we scream with delight. And I always look at my mum and dad, his arms around her from behind, leaning his chin on her head, and it makes me feel very lucky.

Later, Nonna Anna tucks me into bed and smothers my forehead with kisses before she starts putting the clothes I've thrown around onto coat hangers. She's in seventh heaven. Stealing one of Mia's children away from her is like a dream come true. My dad stopped belonging to her when my mum came along. I think my father tends to forget anyone else is around when Mia enters the room. My grandmother's disapproval of the way Mia runs the household is very vocal. I shouldn't walk around naked in front of my brother, for example, and nor should my mother. Once in a while my father will make the trip from the bathroom to his bedroom naked, and I can't say it's an attractive picture, but it hasn't traumatized me. It's unnatural, my nonna Anna will say. Why can't we be self-conscious like normal people? she asks.

I've never really been embarrassed by much. I just couldn't be bothered doing things, that's all, an aspect of me that Mia can't cope with. Sometimes I think I do it even more just so she won't win. At this moment, though, I'm willing to give in. To do anything to make her better.

Nonna Anna gives me one more kiss and turns off my bed lamp.

"Tutto a posto," she says, shutting the closet door. *Everything in its place.*

But my family is split into three, and no one is in their place.

Chapter 8

I LOOK FOR Luca at lunchtime to see how he's coping at my aunt's place. He's looking miserable by the cafeteria, and when he sees me, his little face lights up, which makes me want to cry.

"Are you having fun?" I ask over-cheerfully.

"Mummy's having a nervous breakdown," he says, and I can tell he has no idea what it is.

"Have you got your lunch?" I ask, fixing up his tie and socks because the administration around here are Nazis about such things.

"That's what Anthony says has happened to Mummy."

"Doesn't Anthony still believe in Santa Claus? Doesn't that prove that Anthony doesn't know much?"

Mr. Brolin walks by and stops beside us. "Seniors' lunch area is on the roof."

"Can I just finish speaking to my brother?"

He gets me on an answering-back call and I get another afternoon of detention. I can't even open my mouth to plead my case. Any attempt is construed as answering back.

Luca looks at me helplessly and I can sense he's close to tears.

"I'll ring you," I say, "and then maybe we can talk to Zia Teresa about Pinocchio staying over."

"Promise."

"Cross my heart, hope to die." My voice cracks as I say that. And he hears that crack, and I know it kills him a bit inside.

The day gets worse. We have drama, and for me, drama class is a four-times-a-week nightmare. Every lesson Mr. Ortley puts on a piece of music and asks us to dance, and every lesson we stare back at him, some of us with disinterest, others with horror. Nobody ever dances. Nobody but him. He dances like a maniac, which is a bit embarrassing because he's about fifty, and seeing a fifty-year-old dancing to Limp Bizkit is pretty nauseating.

"If you can't lose your inhibitions, you'll never be able to convince a crowd of people that you're someone else. That's what you have to do as an actor," he says between breaths.

As usual, no one moves.

"Mr. Mackee? Are you going to grace the dance floor with your moves?"

Thomas Mackee gives a snort, which is kind of like a no.

"And you did drama for what reason?"

"Because I thought it would be an easy pass, sir. And you went to the National Institute of Dramatic Art for what reason?"

Ortley doesn't care. He seems to like what he does. He tells us that he's waiting for one of those perfect teaching moments when he can say it's all worth it and then he'll quit.

"Miss Spinelli?"

I'd love to do the snort thing, but it would give Thomas Mackee too much satisfaction.

"I'd rather not."

"Why?"

"Because it'll make me feel self-conscious," I lie.

"Why?"

I shrug and look down.

I've perfected the art of shyness. I had three years of practice at Stella's, and it's brought me great comfort over the years. When I was being my un-shy self, I got a different sort of spotlight. Not the one I wanted. I got detentions, was tested for hyperactivity, ridiculed, hassled, ostracized. By the time my Stella friends came to save me, I was ripe for it. Ready to go into some kind of retirement. Because it gets pretty exhausting being on the perimeter.

Here in drama, I don't actually care what people think of me, and deep down I'm not really self-conscious. I just don't have the passion for this or the drive. I would like to go onto autopilot for the whole of Year Eleven drama. It's not as if we're going to be able to perform this year.

"Are you scared people will make fun of you?"

This man does not give up. He looks me straight in the eye when he speaks to me. No one in this school has done that all year except William Trombal, and that was to intimidate me.

"Maybe," I mumble.

"You want to dance."

"You want me to dance?"

"No. *You* want to dance. Every time the music comes on, you sway."

Everyone's looking at me.

"It's instinct."

"Then act on instinct rather than on what other people think," he says in a flat, hard voice.

He turns away from me dismissively. It's as if he couldn't be bothered.

My mother forced me to take drama. "You'll be in your element," she said.

"She's shy," my dad tried to explain.

"Yes, in her left toe she's shy. She's just lazy. That's her problem. She's too busy worrying about what her friends—"

"I don't care what my friends think."

"You care what they'll do when they remember that you're the one with personality."

"Is it okay if I have a say over what *I* want?" I asked.

"That's the problem, Frankie. Once you start hanging out with them, they don't give you a say."

"You just want me to be like you," I shouted.

"You *are* like me. Get used to it," she shouted back.

My father would go around and shut all the windows in the kitchen so the neighbors couldn't hear us shouting, but Mia and I would go at it until I backed down or my dad would say, "Mia, she's a kid. Couldn't you just let her win for once?"

But it was never in Mia's makeup to back down.

"Is that what you want, Frankie? That I let you win?"

Yes, I'd want to scream. *Just once, let me win.*

We'd go to bed furious with each other, and then she'd wake me in the middle of the night and come and lie on my bed and we'd talk for hours, about nothing and everything, and she'd let me touch the scars on her stomach—the scars from where they cut me out of her.

"My pelvis was too small," she'd say, "and you were in such a hurry to come out that they had to deliver you by Cesarean, and by the time I woke up from the anesthetic, Nonna Anna and Nonna Celia had already held you, and I felt so cheated and I said to your father, 'Let's always take care of her, Robert. No one else is to take care of her but you and I.'"

But here I am at my grandparents' house, knowing that this is killing Mia more than a breakdown. And I need to get myself back home, and Luca too. Because if we don't, my mother will feel as if we've been ripped from her without the anesthetic, and the pain waves will be felt by all of us.

I need to get back. But I don't know how.

My detention with Mr. Brolin means that I have to come into contact with Jimmy Hailler again. He gives me a wave, as if we're long-lost friends, and I ignore him. So he turns his attention to some Year Eight kid next to him, who is looking over at Mr. Brolin, frightened of being caught speaking. The kid looks miserable. Not just Brolin miserable or Jimmy Hailler miserable, but it's there in his eyes and Jimmy Hailler doesn't make things any better.

Later, I sit under the tree in Hyde Park: it's one of those fantastic weather days that bring everyone out, and I sit among strangers enjoying the sun and watching the old guys play on the giant chess game. I like this park. It's full of life. Of greenies selling points of view, of lovers lying on the grass smooching, of Japanese tourists having their photo taken in front of the fountain, of the cathedral looming over us. At this time of the afternoon, there are no Sebastian kids around and I feel a bit at peace.

I see the Year Eight kid from detention walking as fast as possible down the pathway, and sure enough, there's Jimmy Hailler trailing him. A fury builds up inside of me. I don't know what comes over me, but I'm up on my feet and walking toward him before I can talk myself out of it.

"You should be ashamed of yourself."

He looks around, to see if I'm speaking to someone else.

"Are you talking to me?"

"Yes I am, Mr. Taxi Driver, De Niro. You're a bully and I know you don't care, but I just thought you should know that I think you're scum. He's probably some miserable kid with his own demons and he doesn't need yours."

I'm actually shouting, and I feel as if there are tears in my eyes, but I don't care. I'm just sick of all the misery—my absolute lack of control over everything. For a moment, I catch a glimpse of shock on his face, but I walk away. When I reach the lights on Elizabeth Street, I find that he's next to me.

"It's my favorite film, you know." He's got a lazy voice that comes across as an annoying drawl.

At first I ignore him.

"*Taxi Driver,*" he persists.

"Of course it is," I say, because it's just too much effort to ignore him. "And I bet I can tell you what your second-favorite film is."

He gives me one of those go-ahead-but-you'll-be-wrong looks, and the lights change and I walk away. But after a moment I turn back, feeling challenged. He's still standing at the lights.

I reach him, my arms folded, and I know I'm going to be right and I am as smug as he is. *"Apocalypse Now."*

No reaction.

"I'm right, aren't I? I can tell."

He doesn't give an inch, so I walk away for the second time.

"So what's your favorite?" he yells out. *"The Sound of Music?"*

He catches up to me.

"I'm not as easy to work out as you are," I tell him as we walk past Market Street.

"It is. I can tell. You love *The Sound of Music.*"

"No I don't."

"You've watched it fifteen times. You've jumped around a gazebo pretending you're sixteen going on seventeen. You've sung 'My Favorite Things' when you're sad, and every time Captain von Trapp's voice catches during 'Edelweiss,' you bawl your eyes out."

I stop and look at him, ready to deny it, but then I feel my mouth twitching. "Seems like I've watched it one or two times less than you have," I say.

"Think about it," he tells me as we sit in Starbucks, soaking marshmallows into our hot chocolates. "*Empire* magazine will interview you one day and you're going to admit that it's your favorite movie. At least I'll come across dark and mysterious."

"Do you know how many guys would pick *Taxi Driver* and *Apocalypse Now* as their favorite films? You'll come across as a cliché."

"I like *The Princess Bride* as well."

"If you spread that around, you just might get lucky with the girls."

"What makes you think that I'm not lucky with them now?"

I make a scoffing sound. "Dream on."

"Bitch."

"Just honest."

After a moment he nods as if agreeing.

"So what do you girls talk about?"

"Nothing exciting. You guys most of the time."

"What's the Eva Rodriguez chick like?"

"She's pretty cool," I say. "What is it about her that makes everyone interested? There are better-looking girls."

He shrugs. "Good-looking, knows her sports, uncomplicated. Doesn't have to prove a point a thousand times a day. Like you said, cool. Maybe even Siobhan Sullivan and Anna Nguyen too." He looks at me almost reprimandingly. "The guys think you need a personality."

"That's actually funny, coming from the Personality Kings of the Western World."

"You do a pretty good act," he says.

"What?"

"The Miss Mute thing."

"I just haven't got anything to say."

"Yeah you do. You kind of mutter it under your breath when you think people can't hear."

"Really."

"Do you want to hang out? At your place or something?"

Hanging out with Jimmy Hailler will mean that I have to say hello to him every day. I'm not ready to say hello to him every day. Too much commitment. It's bad enough that I'm sharing chocolate brownies with him. I shake my head.

"Not today."

"Whenever."

He's the foulest-mouthed boy I've ever come across and constantly uses the c-word. I tell him it offends me and he calls me a prude. I shrug. So be it. I'm a prude. But he says he'll hold back when he's around me. He talks about smoking dope, probably a lot more than he actually smokes it, and just when you think you've come up with some theory about him, he'll make you change your mind. He's obsessed with fantasy fiction and is incredibly biting about those who get fantasy and sci-fi mixed up. The constant Machiavellian grin on his face is a cover-up for some kind of yearning, which doesn't excuse him for being rude and obnoxious and cruel, but he's honest, and I think that deep down he's as lonely as I am.

On the trip home on the bus, I'm vomiting out words, unable to hold them back no matter how hard I try—talking film and music and books and gossip and DVD commentaries and clothing and teachers and students and pets and brothers and loves and hates and lyrics and God and the universe and our dads.

But not mothers.

"That's off-limits," he tells me, and I can't help feeling relieved and guilty.

But most of all, I feel a little less empty than the day before.

Chapter 9

IT'S THURSDAY AFTERNOON, and we have sports. These are the choices for the girls: watching an invitational cricket game; studying in one of the classrooms; or watching the senior rugby league. As you can imagine, I'm torn.

William Trombal is standing on the platform of the bus in his league shorts and jersey as I step on.

"What are you doing?"

He's speaking to me. There is something on his face I can't recognize. It looks a bit like panic and I'm confused.

"Going to the rugby game," I explain politely.

"I think you'll enjoy the cricket."

"Based on the match fixing and controversial rotating roster, I'm ideologically opposed to cricket."

I try to step past him, but he goes as far as putting his arm across to block me. A you're-not-going-anywhere arm.

"Is there a problem here?" Tara Finke asks, pushing forward. He has no choice but to let us on.

I get a glare the whole way there. I don't know what it is with this guy. One minute he's totally conceited, next minute there's a bit of sympathy, then there's the hostility, and today there's everything, including a bit of anxiousness.

I've got to give the Sebastian boys this. They've got heart. But skill? After watching them play, I feel a whole lot better about the basketball game. They get so thrashed that even Tara Finke is yelling, "This is an outrage!"

But they never give in, not once, and half the time I think they're bloody idiots and the other half I can't help cheering if they even touch the ball. The score is too pitiful to divulge. The other side are kind of bastards and our guys are bleeding and, strangely enough, every single time William Trombal gets thumped by those Neanderthals, my heart beats into a panic.

On the way back to school, I sit facing him and he's in his own miserable world. I actually think he wants to cry, but that revolting male protocol of not crying when you feel like shit just kicks in. He looks at me for a moment, and I feel as if I should be nice and look away, but I don't.

"Why don't you just stick to what you're good at?" I find myself asking.

"I warned you," he says gruffly.

"You didn't say there was going to be blood."

"You should have gone to the cricket game."

"Do they win?" I ask.

"Every time."

"Then why don't you join the cricket team?"

He's horrified. "It's not about winning!"

We approach the school, and the first of the guys shuffles past and pats William Trombal on the back. He's their leader, although half their size.

"Maybe next week we'll be able to score, Will."

"You played a great game," one says.

"No, mate, you did."

"No. *You* did, mate."

They go on forever. It's nauseating stuff, but there's no blaming. They get off the bus smiling tiredly.

Oh God, don't let me like these guys.

In legal studies, we debate refugees, because Mr. Brolin hasn't prepared a lesson and he wants us to do the work. Based on our detention relationship, he always calls on me, and on principle I refuse to give in.

"What's your opinion, Miss Spinelli?" he asks (he pronounces it spin-a-lee). He does the stare that doesn't intimidate any of us. It almost makes me want to laugh out loud.

"What's *your* opinion, Mr. Brolin?" Tara Finke asks.

She gets into trouble for speaking without putting up her hand.

"What *I* think isn't the issue, Miss Finke."

"Why?" she persists.

I can guarantee he won't give his opinion. He sits on the fence in the name of professionalism and gets someone else to voice his fascist views (I've got to stop sitting next to Tara Finke), and around here, there's always a candidate.

"Why should we let people in who jump the line?" Brian Turner asks. He's unimportant in the scheme of things, but he would be so shocked if someone pointed out his unimportance to him.

"Because in their country there mightn't be a line," Tara Finke says.

"They just want to come here because we're the land of plenty," this girl who always states the obvious says, stating the obvious.

"Yeah, plenty of bullshit," Thomas Mackee mutters under his breath. Tara Finke and I look at him, surprised, while Brolin comes stalking down the aisle to write in Thomas Mackee's diary for language.

"I agree with Thomas," Tara Finke says.

Thomas Mackee looks horrified. "Don't."

"Don't what?"

"Don't agree with me." He looks around at his friends, and with his finger twirling around his head, he makes the "she's cuckoo" sign. They snicker with him.

"We have a responsibility," she continues without missing a beat.

"What? To let terrorists into the country?" Brian Turner asks.

"I thought we were talking refugees, not terrorists," Thomas Mackee says.

"See, you agree with me," Tara Finke argues.

"I *do not* agree with you. I just don't agree with them," he says, rolling his eyes.

"In what way don't you agree with me?" she snaps. "We're saying the same thing. That there's plenty of bullshit here and that refugees aren't terrorists."

Brolin grabs Tara's diary to record the "bullshit" because it gives him a purpose.

"We're the only democratic country in the world that puts

children in jail," she says, looking around at everyone.

"It's very easy to express outrage from your comfortable middle-class world, Miss Finke," Mr. Brolin says, pleased with himself.

"Well, that's pretty convenient," she says sarcastically. "Shut the comfortable middle class up and rely on the fact that the uncomfortable lower classes in the world aren't able to express outrage and offer solutions. They're too busy trying not to get killed."

"I don't like your tone," he says.

"My tone's not going to change, Mr. Brolin."

"You have to question where you get your facts from," Brian Turner says.

"Where do you get yours? The *Telegraph? Today Tonight?* Your parents? Well, my mum works for the Red Cross Refugee and International Tracing Agency, and she goes and visits the people in Villawood every two weeks. We don't put on our uniforms just when it suits us, and I resent someone stopping me from saying what I believe just because I live happily in the suburbs."

Mr. Brolin looks uncomfortable. He's saved by the bell, and he's out of there before we even pick up our books.

Ryan Burke, a guy from my English preliminary extension class, approaches us, smiling.

"We're trying to get a social-justice group thing happening around here," he tells us. "You interested?"

"Sounds cool," Tara says.

"Oh shucks. Wish I belonged," Thomas Mackee snickers as he passes by with his posse.

"Ignore him," Ryan Burke says, walking alongside us. "He's just trying to rebel. His mother's high up in antidiscrimination."

"That should come in handy when he gets discriminated against for not having a brain," Tara says before leaving us for her design and technology class.

We're outside our English preliminary extension room and end up sitting together.

I like Ryan Burke and his group. They can be cool and take their work seriously at the same time. Even the slackers like them, although once or twice there'll be a dig about their dedication. These guys feel just as comfortable surfing as they do going to the theater. They like girls but don't feel the need to date them, and at first they were the hardest to get to know because they had so many female friends from outside the school. More than anything, they enjoy each other's company, and although there is a lot of tension between them because of their competitiveness, they're the type of guys you like to see around the place.

Ryan Burke is good-looking. He has that golden-haired look, with a gorgeous smile. I think he hates the perception that he's the good old boy, and once in a while he rebels against the image. But deep down he has a decency that I think will stay with him.

He becomes my English extension companion. Like Shaheen from biology and Eva from economics, our relationship is confined to sitting next to each other in class and whispering. In the halls and on the quadrangle we acknowledge each other, but there is no need for in-depth chatting. The bonding takes place in class.

In English extension, we're doing an Austen unit, and Ryan and I analyze who we are in *Pride and Prejudice*.

"I'd like to think I'm Darcy," he says, "but I think I'm a bit of a Bingley. I can be talked out of things sometimes. You?"

"I'd like to think I'm Elizabeth, but deep down I think I'm the one whose name no one can remember. Not Lydia the slut or Mary the nerd or Jane the beauty or Elizabeth the opinionated. I'm the second-youngest. The forgotten one."

"Yeah, I know which one you're talking about. What's-her-name."

"Yeah."

Later, I walk down the senior corridor and William Trombal is coming from the opposite direction, speaking to his friends. They're having one of those Trekkie-versus-Trekker discussions. There's just something about William Trombal that screams out *Star Trek* fan. I personally can't do the Vulcan salute with my fingers and have felt inferior because of it, so disliking William Trombal more than ever suits me just fine. He's laughing at something one of them says, and it transforms him completely. It's the first time I've ever seen him smile, and it's kind of devastating. They walk by me, completely oblivious. Until the very last moment, when he looks over at me and our eyes hold for a moment or two.

And I get this twitch in my stomach.

I walk through Grace Bros. to get through to George Street to catch my bus, and I find myself going straight to the counter that sells my mother's favorite perfume. I spray it in the air and it's as if the scent's a genie and it triggers everything off inside me and I can't get over what comes up with that one spray. Memories and photos and sayings and advice and music and lectures and shouting and security and love and nagging and hope and despair . . . despair . . . why has despair come up? I don't remember despair in her life, but it is evoked with this magical spray. But more than anything, I remember passion.

I look around for the counter that sells my scent, but I'm so petrified that if I spray it in the air, nothing will come out. And then Mia's scent seems to fade away and everything else fades away with it and I know that all I have to do to recapture it is press the spray button again.

But I don't.

Later, my dad picks us up from Nonna's and Zia Teresa's and takes us home for the afternoon. We lie on their bed, and my mum is holding on to us so tight that I can't breathe. She holds us and she's crying and she says, "I'm sorry, I'm sorry, I'm sorry," over and over again until I can't bear the sound of those words.

And I want to tell her everything. About Thomas Mackee the slob and Tara Finke the fanatic and Justine Kalinsky the loser and Siobhan Sullivan the slut. And I want to tell her about William Trombal and how my heart beat fast when he looked at me, but more than anything, I want to say to her that I've forgotten my name and the sound of my voice and that she can't spend our whole lives being so vocal and then shut down this way. If I had to work out the person I speak to the most in a day, it's Mia, and that's what I'm missing.

My nonna comes in, and I feel her gently pull the skirt of my school uniform down over my thighs because my underpants are showing. I bury my face in my mum's neck and I inhale her scent as they pull me gently away from her. I inhale it with all my might so I can implant it in my mind.

Because I need it to be my badge.

Chapter 10

IN HISTORY CLASS, I'm sandwiched between Thomas Mackee and Justine Kalinsky. None of his friends are in this class, so he doesn't feel the need to be Neanderthal man, although our history teacher has explained that Neanderthal man was very misunderstood and not the boofhead he was reputed to be. As usual, Thomas Mackee is making those frustrated grunting noises that have nothing to do with the Franco-Prussian War. He does what he always does in his spare time. He tries to decipher musical notes from some tabular form. Thomas Mackee has a passionate need to be in a punk band, but from the looks of things he learned music by ear, and now, for some reason, he has to know how to read it. When I can stand it no longer, I grab the book and sheet in front of him and pass them to Justine Kalinsky so quickly that they are undetected by the teacher and Thomas Mackee can't get to them.

It takes Justine Kalinsky ten minutes to decipher the notes. She's like this music genius. I hand the music back to him, and he makes one of those grunts that Cheetah makes in Tarzan movies when

Tarzan explains something important to him. A kind of "huh" and "oh yeah" mixed into one.

I look at him. "Would you like me to introduce you to her? Her name's dumb bitch."

"Why don't you just take a Midol," he snarls.

I ignore him, and as we pack up he grunts a thanks to Justine, who glances at me, distressed.

"This doesn't mean we have to be his friend, does it?"

On the bus, Justine Kalinsky and I sit in the back row making small talk about one of the teachers. When the bus stops at Broadway, about ten Pius girls get on. Two of them are Michaela and Natalia, my Stella friends. As usual, they're animated, enjoying their lives with those around them. Why do I feel as if something's missing in my life without them and they don't feel the same about me? That doesn't make them bad, does it? My mother's voice goes through my head. She's the hoarder of memories. "Remember the time they stayed for the weekend and didn't even say thank you or goodbye? Remember the time they wouldn't come to the phone when you were crying and apologizing about something you had no reason to be sorry for? Remember the times they'd come to school and decide they weren't going to speak to you that day?" No, Mum. Because I chose not to remember the moments that pigeonhole me as one of the top five losers of all time, but hey, thanks for the memories.

Natalia and Michaela spot me instantly. "Oh my God," they scream, running down the aisle, knocking people in the face with their bags. Thomas Mackee looks up from the music magazine he's reading, unimpressed by the squealing. I don't think it's the excitement of seeing me as much as the theatrical aspect of their personalities that compels them to do it. But they always made me laugh at St. Stella's. They gave me some identity.

We hug, and a few of the other ex–Stella girls wave from the front of the bus. Others ignore me. Girls like Tina, our archenemy, who'd throw a party and invite everyone in my group but me. The girls would always tell me not to take things personally, but I never believed there was any other way of taking it. Thankfully, they'd be loyal and not go to whatever I wasn't invited to, except when they couldn't get out of it.

"So how's life with the Sebastian boys?"

They tend to ask the same question each time I see them. Thomas Mackee hears the question and turns around, eyebrows raised as if to say, "Go on, what are we like?"

"Pretty pathetic. Well, the Year Elevens, anyway," I say, giving him a look back. "You?"

"Waverley guys are okay."

"Are you going to that party?" one of the Pius girls behind us asks them.

They have an animated discussion about who is going to be there and who isn't and what they're not going to wear. Then they remember that I'm there.

"Who do you hang out with?" Natalia asks, looking over my shoulder. She's always done that. Wherever you are, whoever you are, she'll always look over your shoulder to see if there's someone more exciting to speak to. It used to make me feel paranoid.

I don't answer. They haven't noticed Justine Kalinsky. They never noticed her at Stella's either, except to make fun of her.

"I rang the other night," I tell Michaela, changing the topic.

"Really. Did you leave a message?"

"Kind of."

"Is everything okay?"

I feel awkward with Justine sitting next to me. She takes out a music book and studies it intently.

"My mum's sick," I say in a hushed tone, turning my body to face them so Justine Kalinsky doesn't hear.

"Oh my God, Francis. Is she okay?"

I look at them and I don't know what to say. It's the first time I've said it out loud, and I find I can't really describe what Mia has. People want symptoms. They want physical evidence. This thing my mum has is like the *X-Files*. It can't be explained to the non-believer, and I'm just not ready to describe it at all right now. Not to someone who's looking over my shoulder.

Thankfully, the dreaded Tina is walking down the aisle. I'm about to snicker something to the girls, but she arrives first.

"We're getting off at the Forum for coffee," she says before walking away, and I realize she's speaking to Michaela and Natalia.

"Cool," Natalia says.

This time it's my turn to look over their shoulders. "You hang out with Tina? We hate Tina."

"We hang out with everyone," Natalia says defensively.

"She's a bitch."

"Once you get to know her, she isn't."

What is it with that argument? Why is it that you have to jump through hoops of fire to find out that someone's decent? The fact that someone is a bitch on the surface says heaps about them.

"She treated us like dirt."

"No she didn't. She only treated you that way. You take things too personally, Francis. You always have."

Justine's stop approaches and she presses the button. She bumps past me, but I'm still looking at them.

"Come for a coffee with us," they plead. "We haven't spoken for ages."

They look as if they mean it.

"Another time," I tell them, and I get off the bus with Justine. I just don't want to be on the bus for another second. Justine doesn't ask why I'm following her home. Justine Kalinsky never questions anything. She doesn't even look smug. She just walks, her bag bumping against her hip, her ginger hair coming out of its clasp.

"Are you okay?" she asks after a while.

"Just having one of those days."

"No. I mean are you okay in general? You don't seem to be. You haven't all term."

It's the most we've ever spoken. I don't want to be her bosom buddy and I don't want to tell her about my mum.

"It's just Sebastian's getting to me," I half-lie. "At least the Pius girls seem to be having a better time than us."

"I'm having a great time."

I glance at her.

"No, it's true," she says, "compared to Stella's. I hated Stella's."

"Then what about all the protest Tara Finke goes on about? Why do you go along with her if you love the place?"

"Because she has every right to. It's unfair what we have to put up with there. But that doesn't make me hate the school. It's better than complaining about nothing or discussing the tragic return of the off-the-shoulder T-shirt," she says, referring to Natalia and Michaela's conversation and revealing a bit of a bitchy streak. Which I kind of like.

After a while, I ask, "What was wrong with Stella's? We had nothing to complain about."

She shrugs. "Yes we did. People just convinced you that we didn't."

" 'You,' singular or plural?"

She looks at me. "You think people chose not to hang out with me, don't you? But it was my choice. I chose not to hang out with them. The only people I wanted to hang out with, I'm getting to hang out with now."

I realize she's including me in these "people."

"Me?"

"I think it's because you were a bit of a dickhead like the rest of us in music, but we kind of never knew it until we went to music camp in Year Nine for elective. I'd never seen you without your friends, and you were so different. So *loud*. And I thought, who is she? You were such a show-off, for three days, and everyone shit-stirred you and you let them, which was so much fun. And you sang 'On My Own' from *Les Mis* and you weren't even self-conscious and it blew everyone away. I reckon that's why Ms. Tagar picked it for the musical in Year Ten. Except you didn't go for it."

"I'm not into musicals."

"Really? Funny that you knew all the words to all the songs."

She turns into a tree-lined street of massive Federation houses and already I feel calmer.

Suddenly, Justine Kalinsky gasps and pulls me behind a tree.

"Oh my God. The tuba guy."

"The what?" I ask, trying to look through the branches.

"Don't look. He'll think we're looking," she whispers.

We both look ridiculous.

"Let's try to act natural."

"Hiding behind a tree?"

She puts a finger to her lips and we stay hidden until I feel a giggle build up inside of me. A guy wearing a Sydney Boys High uniform walks by holding a tuba.

Justine's face goes the most ferocious shade of red, and the moment he's five steps away she grabs my hand and we run in the opposite direction.

We don't stop running until we reach the top of the street, leaning on someone's front fence, taking massive breaths.

"Who's the tuba guy?"

"I don't know his name."

"How long have you not known him?"

She looks at me miserably. "You're going to think I'm a loser."

"Justine, my friends from Stella's are hanging out with a girl who once wrote 'Francis Spinelli's mum is a lesbian slut' on a wall at Petersham station. I think you'll just have to wait for that Loser of the Month tiara a little while longer while I wear it, with pride, around my neighborhood."

"Tina was always jealous of you."

"You're avoiding the question."

"Three years. I'm in the same combined school band with him."

"Have you ever spoken to him?"

"He looks at me at the bus stop. Sometimes I'm on the bus and it drives past his stop and we have eye contact."

I think about it for a moment. "I had a bus-stop relationship for four years at Stella's."

"What's his name?" she asks.

"The Boy from the Bus Stop. I never actually spoke to him, but we had a visual relationship, if you know what I mean."

"I think 'Tuba Guy' is a bit more original than that."

"I once liked a guy whose name was Roller Boy because I saw him on Rollerblades, but never found out his name. Then there was Altar Boy, whose name I discovered was Dudley, but I prefer to remember him as the former."

She stops in front of her house and we're awkward for a moment.

"Do you want to come in?"

I shake my head. "I still have to take another two buses home."

"Don't you live in Annandale?"

"I'm staying with my grandparents in Concord. My mum's kind of sick."

She nods, understanding.

I'm about to walk away when I think of something.

"Was I cruel? At Stella's."

She shakes her head. "You just seemed kind of . . . I don't know . . . You always belonged to a big group, but it was like you didn't want to be with them and I couldn't understand why you stayed."

"I liked . . . like them," I explain. "They're my friends."

"I didn't say it was them you didn't like."

I feel as if I'm talking to my biographer and the mood is too dramatic.

"I think you're wrong, though," I tell her.

"About?"

"The return of the off-the-shoulder T-shirt. Be afraid of that. *Be very afraid.*"

She giggles. I grin. I go home to my grandparents feeling okay.

Chapter 11

ONCE A MONTH, my nonna has the Rosary at her place. About twenty people, male, female, mostly over sixty, mostly Italian-speaking, invade the house, their voices rising above each other as if they're arguing rather than just greeting. I've promised my nonna that I'll make the coffee while they're saying the Rosary, placing it in the giant thermos to keep it hot. The guests hand me various selections of cakes and slices for the after-Rosary gossip fest, and I arrange them onto trays while my nonna sits every-one down in the living room. Just before they're ready to begin, the doorbell rings. A moment later I watch my nonna freeze as a woman stands in front of her, haughtily holding out a plate of biscuits.

S biscuits.

Nonna's famous S biscuits.

And I know instantly it's William Trombal's grandmother.

I take the plate off her politely and walk into the kitchen and begin to make the coffee. It takes forever to make enough for twenty, and I just want to get into my pajamas and curl up in bed.

While I wait for the coffee to come up, I stand at the door and watch them praying, concentrating especially on Nonna and William Trombal's grandmother. Through the Joyful Mysteries they're putting on a front of piety, but by the Sorrowful Mysteries things have deteriorated. I can actually see my nonno looking at my nonna warningly and doing that twisting lip thing with his fingers, and I see the superiority on William Trombal's grandmother's face. The same air of superiority that I've seen on his.

And at that exact moment, I realize that the S biscuits must go. They cannot be paraded around by that smug woman while people congratulate her on how smooth the chocolate on top tastes and how perfect they are for dipping into your coffee.

So during the Glorious Mysteries, I put them in the bin, wrap up the garbage bag, and take it outside. I know the Virgin Mary will understand. The Jews are a lot like the Italians, so I'm sure there were jealousy issues between her and the other women of Nazareth.

Then I change into my pajamas and go to bed, trying to get into my English novel.

Half an hour later the doorbell rings. The Rosary group is making such a racket in the living room that no one hears and it rings again.

I go to answer it and find myself face to face with William Trombal. I'm not sure who's more embarrassed, but I figure it's me because of the Harry Potter pj's I'm wearing, courtesy of Luca last Christmas. William looks confused.

"Do you live here?"

"No."

I'm not interested in elaborating, so we leave it at that.

"I'm picking up my grandmother."

"They're still having coffee."

We stand there nodding at each other.

"Can you tell her I'll be waiting in the car?"

"I think you should tell her yourself."

"Maybe I should just wait out here."

He sits on the front porch, and I have no choice but to sit there with him. No matter who his grandmother is, my nonna would be furious if I left him outside on his own.

I'm racking my brains for something to say. He's tapping his leg, pretending that my nonna's garden is the most fascinating he's ever seen.

"It's good of you to run around after your grandmother," I tell him.

He nods. He thinks he's fantastic too.

"I'm her favorite. Youngest grandson and all. You know how Italians are about all that stuff."

The girls in my family have always been the favorites, so no I don't, I'd like to say.

"You don't look Italian," I tell him.

"Half."

"Which half?"

He thinks for a moment, and I see a ghost of a smile appear on his face. "The pigheaded side."

"I thought you said you were only half Italian?"

He bursts out laughing. It's short, as if he's regretted allowing me to make him laugh, but the satisfaction's already mine.

"Do you live around here?"

"Kingsgrove," he says.

"That's miles away."

"She has nine grandchildren. We take turns staying with her and it's my week. You?"

"Annandale."

We nod again, and I suddenly know how teachers feel when they're trying to get information from us. After a moment he turns to face me, leaning his back against the pillar.

"You don't seem to like Sebastian's."

"Why do you say that?"

"You just seem . . . down around the place."

I shrug. "It's being new and all. You've just forgotten what it's like to be new."

"No I haven't. But I kind of know what you're saying. I've been at that place since Year Five, you know. I was a choirboy, like your brother."

"You don't sing for the cathedral choir anymore?"

"No. Just the school one. My voice broke and now I do a very average baritone. *Very devastating*," he says dramatically, but in a way I can tell he means it.

"So what do you want to do next year?"

"Civil engineering. New South Wales University. No matter how high my marks are."

It's strange speaking to someone who is stressed by the idea of getting high High School Certificate marks. But I like the fact that he's scared that those same high marks may get in the way of something he seems to be passionate about doing.

"You?" he asks.

"I haven't the faintest clue. I dread next year, when I'll be asked a thousand times a week."

"That's a bit of an exaggeration. You only get asked one hundred times."

He looks relaxed. As if he's enjoying himself.

"So about that list," he says. "I don't get number nine. What does 'Stalag 17 is a travesty of co-educational drama' mean?"

I can't believe he knows it by heart.

"The girls say they need participation," I inform him. "It's not just about sports, either. They didn't even audition us for drama or debating or anything. They stuck with the preexisting teams."

"It's kind of hard to explain, but people didn't like you girls coming in. Teachers, students, parents. They wanted things to stay the way they were, because the way they were worked. You've been here not even two terms. In drama, for example, don't push for something this year, push for next year's production."

"Fair enough. I'll put it forward to the committee," I say, pretending that we actually have one.

"How come you always do the asking?" he asks.

"Because they think William Trombal and I are like this," I say, crossing my fingers.

Before he can respond, we hear a sound behind us and turn just as my nonna is politely escorting his nonna out. Signora Trombal gives me an evil look, and our nonnas insincerely kiss each other on both cheeks.

As they walk away, she clutches on to him, whispering something urgently in his ear. When he reaches the gate, he turns around and there's this hint of a smile on his face, and he begins to walk back to me. I'm petrified. She's sending him back to demand the biscuits, and he's enjoying it like hell.

He stops in front of me, silent for a moment, and I'm trying not to give away my fear.

"It's Will, by the way," he says.

I don't ask what he means.

"Not William."

"Okay," I say, relieved.

He goes to walk away but then stops again, and a flash of something comes over his face, like a grimace. "Don't come and watch rugby this week. Please."

"Why? Could it get any worse?"

"We're playing last year's winners . . . plus our winger, Sallo—big guy, big hair?—he's going out with their captain's ex-girlfriend. It's going to be ugly."

"Then you'll need fans."

"So you're a fan, are you?"

I think he's flirting with me and I have this ridiculous grin on my face but I can't help it.

He goes to leave but then stops again. "And just so you know," he tells me. "I *know* you're behind the disappearance of the biscuits."

"Biscuits?"

"My nonna's S biscuits."

"Funny, that. My nonna makes S biscuits too. She's actually the Queen of S Biscuits."

He's trying not to grin.

And I don't know why, but I sit on that step until the last person's gone home and I'm still grinning.

Like someone who has a bit of a crush.

Angelina takes me bridesmaid-dress shopping. Her mother comes along and so does Nonna Anna. Her mother doesn't get on with Nonna Anna because Nonna Anna can't stand anyone who's married to her sons, and Angelina doesn't get on with her mother because, even though Angelina's getting married soon, her mother keeps on inviting Angelina's ex-boyfriend over for dinner, hoping that Angelina's going to forget he was a lying scumbag with a zero IQ. Angelina's mother doesn't like me because she thinks that Luca and I are Nonna Anna's favorites, and I hate Angelina's mother because she once said that my mother should stay home and look after her kids instead of getting another degree, and at the moment I don't like Nonna Anna because she won't let me stay up after 10:30 and I missed out on *Buffy.*

Nonna and Angelina's mother make me try on fourteen dresses. Angelina sits on the other side of the room, shaking her head, mouthing obscenities. The dresses are hideous, and Angelina's wedding is in danger of being hijacked by two very angry women who are only united by their obsession with bright-colored taffeta.

I'm a rag doll, pulled at from each side. The moronic shop assistant tells me I look beautiful, and in the distance, I can see that Angelina has had enough. When they make me try on something that's lilac, with boning in the bodice and something called a sweetheart neckline, she lifts herself from the chair and makes her way toward us.

"Get dressed, Frankie. I'm making the dresses."

"You can't sew," her mother says.

"I'll teach myself."

I put on my jeans and throw the dress at the shop assistant. Angelina takes my hand and we make a run for it.

Later on, we're sitting in a café. She's just smoked her fifth cigarette in an hour.

"Those things are going to kill you."

"My mother will beat them to it, so I may as well enjoy another one."

I try to smile, but I can't.

"Luca reckons that everyone's saying that my mum's had a nervous breakdown as opposed to a 'bit of a breakdown.'"

She looks at me, and I can see there are tears in her eyes. Mia's always been her idol. The number of times Angelina ran away from home when she was a teenager and came and stayed with us are countless.

"They're just words," she says. "People use them to try to explain things they don't understand."

"What would you call it?"

I'm about to hear the truth, because Angelina doesn't lie, and after I hear this truth I won't be able to lie either, and that frightens me to death.

"It's depression, Frankie."

"I don't understand. Sad people with sad lives are depressed. Mia's not one of them."

Angelina takes hold of my hand.

"I think everything's just shut down on her. Maybe for one reason or maybe for a thousand. It's kind of like a grief, and it's not a puzzle that you're supposed to work out on your own, Frankie. But I'll tell you this. Mia is not going to get better being looked after by her mother. You have to find a way of getting back home. For you and Robert and Luca and Mia to get back together—and then you start from there."

"But I don't know how," I whisper, trying not to cry. "I just want to go home and I don't know how."

"Then find a way," she says firmly. "I love Nonna and I love the aunties, but don't let them own this. Don't let Mia wake up from this nightmare and find you guys in pieces. It'll kill her more than anything else."

I see Nonna Anna and Angelina's mum coming toward us. I picture a world of *Who Wants to Be a Millionaire* and no *Buffy*.

I need to find a way home.

Chapter 12

I'VE BEEN AT my nonna's for two weeks and nothing has changed at home. Actually, I think it's worse, but the first casualty of all this is truth.

My dad rings me one morning and tells me to contact Mia's university and ask for the rest of the term off.

"I thought you said she was out of bed," I say almost accusingly, as if my dad's lying.

"She is, but she's not ready to go back. Just ring them and we'll talk about it later."

"Why can't you ring them?"

"Because I'd like you to."

"Papa, they've got degrees, not machetes."

"What's that supposed to mean?"

He sounds harassed. With *me*. Am I the one who's locked herself in the house? Since when do I have to fix things around here?

"We can't keep on telling people that Mummy has the flu."

"Then tell them the truth, Frankie."

The truth? I haven't said the truth out loud yet, and I don't know how to go about doing this. I'm in Year Eleven. I'm sixteen years old. I don't want to call up my mother's boss and tell her she's not coming in for the rest of the term. I don't want to use any of the terminology out loud. I'll say it one thousand times to myself, but I can't say it out loud, because if I do, it means it's real. *Nervous breakdown. Depression. Nervous breakdown. Depression.* Such overused words until it actually happens. How many times has Mia said, "I'm having a nervous breakdown, kids"? How many times have I said I'm depressed? Too many times to count. Nothing close to the reality of it at all.

The depression belongs to all of us. I think of the family down the road whose mother was having a baby and they went around the neighborhood saying, "We're pregnant." I want to go around the neighborhood saying, "We're depressed." If my mum can't get out of bed in the morning, all of us feel the same. Her silence has become ours, and it's eating us alive.

I want to stay in bed for the day and not go to school, but I can't bear the idea of Luca being there alone. So I turn up for second-period English. My teacher, Brother Louis, has set us some study questions based on *Henry IV,* and we work on our own. I hold my pen in my hand, but I don't do the work. I haven't slept all week and I can't even see straight.

Brother Louis stands by my desk and looks over my shoulder. He's in his sixties and knows every text we're studying inside out. I've never met anyone who knows so much about literature. I'm not used to Brothers. At Stella's we didn't even have nuns. But he's the kindest man I've ever met, and he's the only person I do homework for because I couldn't bear it if he was disappointed in me.

"Would you like to go to sick bay?" he asks quietly.

I shake my head.

"Then go to Ms. Quinn's office," he suggests gently.

I collect my books and walk out, and I'm so tired that I feel weepy.

Ms. Quinn is on the phone and beckons me in. I don't know what I'm going to say to her. Brother sent me down because I looked sad?

"Do you want to go to the counselor?" she asks gently. It's as if she knows what's going on and I don't know how, because I couldn't imagine my father ringing up the school and revealing anything. Then I realize it's because of Luca.

"Is my brother okay?"

"I haven't seen your brother. Do you want me to?"

"No."

"Will said you were a bit down."

Oh God. Will Trombal thinks I'm a charity case.

"Can I just lie down?"

"I think the counselor—"

"Please, Ms. Quinn. I'm just tired and I want to lie down and not have to talk."

And that's how I spend my day. Sleeping in Ms. Quinn's office. I think, wouldn't it be great if I could open my eyes and it's six months down the track and everything's back to normal?

But when I open my eyes, it's one day down the track, and for the time being, that seems to be enough.

* * *

During a House meeting the next day, when Will Trombal stands in front of us talking, I'm all ears. Whether it has to do with the night at my nonna's or whatever he told Ms. Quinn, I just can't be indifferent anymore. I *so* don't want to be attracted to him, and the fact that I am surprises me. Sometimes when I get home, I convince myself that I'm just romanticizing anyone who's actually spoken to me, but then I see him the next day and my heart starts beating fast and I can't really kid myself. It's not as if he's good-looking, because he's not. Sometimes he's so plain that he looks bland. But it's his voice and his mannerisms that fill him with some kind of color. I listen to his voice and its resonance hooks me in. The worry lines on his forehead, his expression when he twists his face into a smile, and the way his whole face lights up when he laughs those short bursts of laughter. When he looks at me, he must see an annoyed look on my face because I get the same annoyed look back. That's how I feel. Annoyed that I like him.

When he finishes speaking, Ms. Quinn gets up and gives us a rundown on administrative stuff, and I look over at him and he's looking back. Tara Finke, as usual, is nudging me and muttering comments under her breath. But I don't react. I just keep staring and so does he, until the bell rings and we all file out.

95

chapter 13

A GUY IN Year Twelve has a party and invites all the girls in Year Eleven. No one in our group of four mentions it until the very last minute.

"I don't think I'll go," I murmur to Siobhan when she asks.

"Why not? It's two guys to every girl."

Wow! Two Sebastian guys. Dream come true!

"It'd be good to make an effort," Justine says.

"Maybe," I say with a shrug.

"How would you get there?" Siobhan asks me.

I shrug again. "Probably my father. You?"

"Obviously not my father. He'd probably insist on coming in and giving everyone a Breathalyzer."

Siobhan's father's a cop. He runs the station over at Marrickville and puts the fear of God into those who work under him, especially his family. He liked me in Year Seven. "Make sure she doesn't do anything stupid," he'd tell me. I never liked that about him. Just that certainty he had that Siobhan was always going to do something wrong.

Siobhan gets wasted at parties. It was always the thing you heard about her in Year Ten. She's the type that constantly imagines herself in love with some loser and then she ends up getting shit-faced and crying in the toilet.

When I think about it, my mother was never threatened by Siobhan Sullivan's reputation.

"People with lost personalities will suffer a great deal more than those with lost virginities," she told me one afternoon after Siobhan was suspended from St. Stella's for cutting school in Year Ten and going to the beach with a couple of the St. Paul's guys.

"So you're telling me to go out there and be a slut?"

She looked up from her marking. "Firstly, I'm not telling you to go out there and lose your virginity. I trust that you're not going to do it just because you're hanging out with the Siobhan Sullivans of the world. And secondly, losing your virginity doesn't make you a slut. I slept with your father when I was your age. . . ."

"Mia," my father roared from the other room.

"*What?* So we're going to lie to her now?" she shouted back.

He walked in. "What if your mother finds out? Or my mother?"

"Robert, it was twenty years ago. I don't think there's much they can do."

He looked at me, pointing a finger. "No sex for you." He used the Soup Nazi's accent from *Seinfeld.*

"Stop treating this like a joke," Mia said, irritated.

"You think Frankie having sex is a joke to me?"

"I don't want her to have sex, Rob. I want her to stop hanging around people like Michaela and Natalia, who suck the life out of who she is."

The people I'm stuck with in my life now aren't sucking the life out of me, they just suck. That's what I'd like to say to her.

"I'm not going," Tara says, referring to the party. "I've got better things to do."

"You wish," Siobhan mutters.

"I think we should make an attempt," Justine Kalinsky says. "I've got a piano accordion recital, but it'll be over by eight."

"Don't say that too loud," Siobhan tells her.

"Making fun of the piano accordion thing is a bit passé now, Siobhan," Tara Finke tells her.

"So are you, Tara."

Oh, what a united group we are!

"I'll pick you up, but after that you're on your own," I tell Siobhan. "I'm not spending the night looking for you."

By the time we arrive, everyone is paralytic. Even Will Trombal.

The guy throwing the party is handing out vodka Jell-O shots, and after a couple the sensation is strange.

On the dance floor, Eva Rodriguez is surrounded by a bunch of guys. Her parents are from the Philippines, with the usual Spanish-and-Filipino mix of caramelized skin and almond-shaped eyes. Most of the guys think she's gorgeous, but the Filipino guys adore her. I watch them move. Their bodies are like liquid as they dance. When they walk, dance, play basketball, they all seem to glide to a tempo that the rest of us can't hear or respond to.

Will Trombal sees me from the other side of the room and he grins and he makes a beeline for me and my mind is buzzing with the best opening.

Hi.

Hey.

How's it going?

Great party.

Love your shirt.

Great music.

Crap music.

And he's coming closer and closer and the way he's looking at me makes me think that I'm going to have the most romantic night in the history of my life. I open my mouth to say something and he sticks his tongue down my throat.

We're in a corner, pashing, and I don't even know what's got me to this point. A look in the corridor? A flirt outside my nonna's house? All I know is that no one exists around us. I don't know whether we're kissing for five minutes or five hours and my mouth feels bruised, but I can't let go. Because it feels so good to be held by someone other than Luca. Will's arms tremble as they hold me and his heart beats hard against me and I know that whatever I'm feeling is mutual. For a moment I taste the alcohol on his breath, and it brings me back to reality.

"Do that sober and I'll be impressed," I say before walking away.

Justine Kalinsky is a wallflower all night. I can tell she's itching to dance, but she just stands there and there's a worried, pinched look on her face.

"Siobhan's gone into the bedroom with that Year Twelve guy who's in charge of the microphones, you know, at assembly," she tells me. "They're really drunk."

"Siobhan's a big girl."

"With bad taste in guys."

"Not our problem."

Over the weekend, I think of Will one thousand times a day. I think, what if he doesn't speak to me on Monday? What if he doesn't ask me out? What if my heart beats at this rate for the rest of my life until he does? Why isn't he ringing? He knows I'm at my nonna's place. His nonna would have the phone number.

Oh, ring, ring, why doesn't he give me a call?

And then it hits me. I'm going to ask him out. Except I've never asked a guy out before. Should I wait for him to ring me? He's made it obvious that he's interested, even if he was drunk, so why wouldn't he ring? You don't kiss me the way he kissed me and not mean business. Do guys shake like that with every kiss? I change my mind one hundred times in a minute. Michaela would wait. Natalia would say, "Let him ring you." But I feel as if I've spent my life waiting. For phone calls from my Stella friends. For Mia to be okay. For someone else to decide that it's right for Luca and me to go home.

I'm going to ask Will Trombal out! And for the first time in a month, I can see beyond the next five minutes and what I see doesn't seem so bad.

There's a lot of awkwardness on Monday. Not a lot of eye contact between the sexes. There's a bit of snickering as Siobhan walks by, and Tara looks from the snickerers to Siobhan.

"I'm not going to ask," Tara says.

I'm sitting on my desk, working out my strategy, when Justine Kalinsky approaches us. She has the most distressed look on her face.

"You're going to be devastated," she says.

"About?"

"I don't know if I can tell you."

"Then why bring it up?" Tara Finke asks.

"It's not as if I wanted to overhear it."

"She pashed Will Trombal. And the whole world's talking about it, right?" Siobhan mocks.

"Not even remotely devastating," I say.

"It's much worse than that."

"Can you stop being so dramatic? I don't do devastation," I tell her.

"Will Trombal has a girlfriend."

Oh my God, I am so devastated.

"I think she's devastated."

I try to shake my head. "I'm not. . . ."

"Yes you are."

I don't want to look at them. I don't want to see the I-told-you-so on Tara Finke's face or the you-sucker on Siobhan Sullivan's or the pity on Justine Kalinsky's.

I feel as if my throat is made out of cardboard, and all of a sudden kissing Will Trombal is the most embarrassing thing in the world. I feel like Adam and Eve when God points out to them that they're naked.

I feel tears well in my eyes and I can't even stop them from happening. I can't stop anything from happening in my life. I just want to get through the day, the week, the year, without ever having to see Will Trombal again.

During period five, I'm in class, not listening, looking out the window into the quadrangle, and I see Luca, his head down, walking toward the toilets. I ask to be excused and I wait for him outside and then we find a place, any place, for some kind of time together. Time that's been taken away from us by everyone. We find a corner in the library and we hold on to each other tight and he begins to cry. I feel the sobs racking his body before I hear them. I can cope with my misery, but not Luca's. His pain makes me ache, and I'm crying so much that my whole body is hurting.

"Don't be sad, Luca. Please don't be sad."

And I don't know why I'm saying something so foolishly simple. *Don't be sad.*

Worse still, I realize we're not alone. Thomas Mackee is standing there, staring as if he's come across some alien life forms. He nods in acknowledgment and I nod back. And then he's gone with the secrets of my family's misery locked in his brain, and I wonder when he'll use them as part of his arsenal, part of his repertoire of mockery.

"You know what I think?" Tara Finke says on the bus home. She's the first to say anything to me after I've done a literal rendition of the sound of silence all day.

Don't say it, I want to scream at her. *Don't say anything. Mind your own business, you loser. Don't intellectualize my misery.* Tara Finke knows nothing but words that mean nothing when your insides are in pieces.

"We have an Alanis night."

I look at her, confused.

"Don't be ridiculous," Siobhan Sullivan says. "As if that's going to help. It has to be *Pride and Prejudice.* I've got the whole six episodes."

"I disagree. Food's always good. It always helps," Justine says.

They talk about me as if I'm not there.

"My place," Tara Finke says.

An Alanis night is listening to Alanis Morissette's music, where there's a lot of revenge and anger toward men. We move on to Tori Amos and then Jewel. So much hate and depression is making me feel sick, although that could also be attributed to the Pringles that I sandwiched between two Oreos.

We watch *Pride and Prejudice*. Mr. Darcy is such a hottie that it depresses me because his sideburns remind me of Will Trombal's.

Tara Finke's mother watches it with us. She talks through the whole thing, which gets very tense around the time Colin Firth, aka Mr. Darcy, comes out of his pond, soaking wet.

Tara Finke has had enough. "Mum?" Tara puts a finger to her lips threateningly.

We watch in silence, but I look at the others' faces. All of them glued to the screen, a dreamy look on their faces. A hint of a smile on their lips. A sense of hope. They're all the same. Cynical Tara, couldn't-give-a-shit Siobhan, romantic Justine.

And I want to cry. Because my face looks just like theirs and I haven't felt like anyone else since I was in Year Seven and Siobhan Sullivan and I did the Macarena in the foyer of the chapel and got lunchtime detention for a week.

Justine catches me looking and she smiles, and with tears in my eyes I smile back.

Chapter 14

MY DAD COMES to see me at Nonna Anna's, and we spend the afternoon on the front doorstep in silence. I keep on remembering what Mia asked him once. "Take us away and who are you, Robert?" Worse still, I remember his answer. "Is this a trick question, Mia? Am I dead?" I want to ask him a thousand questions, but somehow we've forgotten how to speak to each other. Does he miss her voice, like I do? Can he remember what she sounds like? Does he not know who he is anymore?

"This is wrong," I tell my dad. "What's happened to Mum isn't right, but Luca and I want to come home."

"She misses you," he says.

"We miss you, Papa. We miss us."

He nods calmly. "Then let's get Luca."

Mia cries when she sees us. Although she's out of bed, she's still in her nightgown, looking a thousand years old. Later, my dad, Luca, and I sit around the table. It's back to the horrible way it was before I went to Nonna's. None of us knowing what to say.

I get the calendar and put it down in front of my dad.

"Wednesday, choir practice," Luca says, clutching on to Pinocchio, who is beside himself with excitement. "Mum picks me up at five o'clock."

"I'll stay after school," I tell them. "On Tuesdays, you have to drop Nonna Anna off at the Italian women's thing."

My dad begins writing. "Next."

"Nonno Salvo has an appointment at the podiatrist every Thursday. Mummy usually takes him."

"And Friday is cemetery day with Nonna Celia."

"Plus Mummy has two conferences this year."

"Frankie, you'll have to ring and cancel them. We can do the rest, but the conferences are going to be out of the question."

"She won't want them canceled. It's taken two years of lobbying to get these conferences."

"What about the shopping?" he asks.

"You do the shopping and we'll work around the rest," I say.

Lots of nods. Lots of determination. And so much doubt that we can't even hide it.

My dad comes home triumphant from his first grocery-shopping assignment. As if he's accomplished God Knows What. I want to remind him that my mum does it every week without fanfare, but I'm too shocked at what he's unpacking.

"What were you thinking?"

"What?"

He looks stunned. A bit hurt. He's just conquered Coles. He feels like he deserves a medal.

"What is this?" I ask, holding up the yogurt.

"Yogurt."

"With six grams of fat per one hundred grams. What happened to nonfat yogurt or ninety-seven percent fat-free yogurt?"

"Are we dieting?"

"Papa, it's not about dieting. It's about keeping our fat intake down. Look at this," I say with a cry in my voice, pulling out some crackers. "What happened to rice crackers, ninety-four percent fat-free as opposed to Chicken in a Biscuit, twenty-two percent fat per one hundred grams?"

By this stage, my dad is looking a bit forlorn, but things only get worse.

"Oh my God!" I hold up the Ice Magic. The stuff you put on ice cream and it hardens like a chocolate top.

"Where did this come from? Do you know what this is? Luca is going to sneak out of bed in the middle of the night and squirt it on his tongue. It's like drugs for ten-year-olds. Today it's Ice Magic. Tomorrow, heroin."

We write out a list that he's to stick to in the future. Luca is already pigging out on the Cheetos and looks disappointed as we eliminate any source of junk food.

I make us dinner and take a big plate in to Mia. It comes back untouched. I throw it away before Luca can see it, and the cycle goes on.

One morning, she's throwing up in the sink. Nothing much, as usual. She's leaning her head against the tap, retching, and the sound becomes as familiar as the music she used to wake us up with. I want to do what she did for me when I was a kid. Hold back my hair and make me cry, not from the feeling of having my guts ripped open, but just from the feeling of being taken care of.

But I stand and I stare. She senses me there and looks for a moment. I don't know what she reads from my face. Am I angry? Sickened? Ashamed?

I want to say, *Please, Mummy, be okay, please be okay, because if you're not okay, we'll never be.*

But I say nothing.

I just go to school.

It's June, about six weeks into the term, and it's getting cold, but they won't let us wear scarves because it's not part of the uniform. I walk through Hyde Park behind the rest of the students, where Luca is running around the fountain with his friends ahead of me, and for a moment there's peace in my heart because he's happy.

After a moment, I realize that I'm not alone. Will Trombal is walking alongside me and I know he's not there by chance. It's been a week since the party. In front of us is Siobhan Sullivan, her arms draped over two boys beside her, her uniform riding up. She lifts herself up and swings her legs in the air.

"I think you should speak to her," he says to me.

"I beg your pardon?"

"There's stuff written about her."

I stop for a moment and look at him. "Would you ask me to speak to a guy about the same thing?"

"Why turn this into a gender issue?"

"Because you made it into one. Would you go up to a guy and warn him if there was stuff written about him?"

"Listen, don't shoot the messenger," he almost shouts. "The shit that's written in the toilets is awful, and if she were my friend I'd talk to her about it."

"Well, it's not in my job description."

"You've made it your job. . . ."

"No I haven't."

"I'm trying to work with you here. . . ."

"No you're not. We haven't got one thing on that list except for that humiliating basketball game, and now you've decided to be Mr. Moral Policeman."

"Forget it," he says, walking away angrily.

"And what's the name for people who kiss other people when they've got a girlfriend?"

He stops and turns around, looking me straight in the eye.

"A weak, spineless prick."

Oh great, I think. *Take the right to call you names right off me, you . . . weak, spineless prick.*

"I've wanted to talk to you about that, but—"

"But what?"

At the moment his face is red, and he's looking at me as if I'm at fault. "It's not as if I planned you," he blurts out.

Planned me?

"Oh, like you *really* plan drunken snogging at parties," I say.

He has the audacity to look hurt.

"Is that all it was to you?" he asks.

"Thinking about it now, yes."

Liar, liar, pants on fire.

"Fine. Then I think I'll stick to my plans in the future. I get results out of my plans."

"Really. Like your rugby game plan? That really works."

"Oh, that's very low. Is that why you come along and watch? To remind me of my failures?"

We don't speak for a moment, but I'm not ready to walk away yet.

"You won't understand about that night," he mutters.

"Try me."

"Okay. I—"

"If you even dare say it was because you were drunk, I can't promise you where this will go."

"Why not? You did. Anyway, I thought I was going to be justifying my actions without you interrupting."

"Then hurry up."

"I don't want you to think I do that all the time," he says, sounding a bit strained.

He's very stressed. I have caused that stress. I am jubilant that I have caused that stress.

"Why would I think otherwise?"

"Because," he says.

Because?

"Don't you do legal studies? Aren't you in mock trial? Does the argument 'because' usually work for you?"

He doesn't even have the decency to be shifty-eyed. He just stares straight at me.

"You were drunk, Will," I say after a moment. "I wouldn't expect you to even remember anything." I turn to go.

"If I was sober, you would have been impressed," he says, repeating my words from that night.

"But you weren't. And I'm not," I say firmly. "And if you think that I am praying at night for you to ask me out, just dream on."

I walk away, so proud of myself that I can hardly contain it.

Dear God, please please please let Will Trombal split up with his girl-friend and ask me out.

The prayer becomes my mantra all night. By 6:30 in the morning my eyes are hanging out of my head and I trudge to the bathroom, half-asleep.

On the way back I pass the living room, where the CDs are lying around on the floor.

They're a combination of my mum's and dad's and mine and Luca's, anything from the Jam to Britney Spears (not mine, I swear to God).

I come across the Whitlams' *Eternal Nightcap,* and it reminds me of being in the car on one of our road trips to the Central Coast, when the four of us would sing the whole way. Our favorite song was "You Sound Like Louis Burdett," and we'd sing it at the top of our voices. My mum would even let us sing the line "All our friends are fuck-ups," and Luca would sing it the loudest because it was the only time we were allowed to swear.

I loved those times on the beach at the end of the day, when the sun was gone and our sunburn would make us shiver in the cool breeze. Luca and I would lie against my parents, licking the salt off their arms, and we'd stay like that until twilight. They're the magical moments I remember. The moments of brown bodies and salt water—

curled hair, of fish and chips on the sand, of sunblock smelling of coconut, of stinging cuts on our feet from jagged rocks, and mostly of the four of us not needing anyone else in the world.

And I remember the nights of listening to their heavy breathing from the other room through the paper-thin walls of the rented house we were in. Listening to their cries and groans.

"Why is Mummy crying?" Luca would ask me.

"Because she's so happy," I'd answer.

I put the CD on and lie back on the carpet, closing my eyes, but then I hear the thumping of running footsteps and I open them to see Luca standing at the door, a look of excitement turning to disappointment, and I know that he would have thought it was my mum.

I beckon him over. "You put one on," I say.

He looks through the collection and then holds one up. "Not until tomorrow, though," he tells me.

My mother's rituals become ours. One morning it's You Am I's "Heavy Heart," and another time my dad puts on Joe Jackson's "A Slow Song," because that was their wedding waltz.

We play Smashing Pumpkins and Shirley Bassey and Jeff Buckley and even Elvis. I try to find music that belongs to me, but I realize that Mia's music has become mine. Mia's everything has consumed us all our lives, and now Mia's nothing is consuming us as well.

After we play our music, we get ready for school, going through the motions, getting on with our lives.

And then the worst thing happens.

I get used to it.

Chapter 15

IN DRAMA, MR. ORTLEY plays "Venus." It's the version by this sixties band, Shocking Blue. And suddenly, out of nowhere, Thomas Mackee starts to dance. Later he tells people that he thought he heard "I'm your penis" rather than "I'm your Venus" and that's why he got up. But, as usual with Thomas Mackee, you never know the truth.

Thomas Mackee on a dance floor is totally uninhibited and hysterical to watch. Despite his lanky slobbiness, he moves well. He makes the most ridiculous faces as he twists, his mouth in an *O* shape, and we're laughing so much our stomachs hurt. He manages to combine the most outrageously physical moves, and they work. At a dance party you wouldn't want to be anywhere near him, but here he has the whole space to himself and he relishes it. I look at Mr. Ortley and he's laughing just as much as we are, and I wonder if this is one of those perfect teaching moments he tells us he's been waiting for.

Thomas Mackee loves music. I can tell by the way his body reacts. For a moment I feel a bit of envy because I think I want to be out there making a fool of myself as well. His rhythm is erratic, and in my head I just can't follow the groove. And then somehow we make eye contact and it clicks.

Don't do it, I tell myself. My ex–Stella friends, like Michaela, would think I was a dickhead. A show-off. A loser. I can just imagine them, exchanging looks that say more than enough. It's how they've stayed popular for so long. By not doing anything that will make them look like fools. They never leave home without their safety nets and I think, good for them, but the thing with safety nets is this. I got tangled in them so many times and the Stella girls always seemed to leave me dangling, upside down, to the point where I almost couldn't breathe anymore.

So I dance.

Thomas makes a *V* with his fingers and he turns it around and points to his eyes as if to say "focus," and I do, matching his moves, swaying to his beat. The guitar arrangement on the song is fun and it's easy to change direction. Everyone is clapping the beat, and there's something so uncoolly cool about it. It's like geographical humor. You just don't get it unless you were there. Thomas Mackee has a sense of the ridiculous and it's contagious, and I'm sure if he were forced to, he'd admit that he's spent a lifetime making up these moves in his bedroom. Was he hiding in there as well? Was he shaking off an image he'd constructed for himself?

He tires, and I catch Siobhan Sullivan's eye and then I take her hand and we're in Year Seven again, making up the moves that made so much sense at the time. There's a recognition in her eyes, and being best friends with her is the most vivid memory I have of St. Stella's, and for one split second I can't remember being friends with anyone else.

At the end we take a bow, and for the rest of the day whenever someone from drama class walks past me in the corridor, it's hard not to grin.

And being that happy makes me feel guilty. Because I shouldn't be. Not while my mum is feeling the way she is. How I can dare to be happy is beyond me, and I hate my guts for it.

I hate myself so much that it makes my head spin.

At times, the house becomes a thoroughfare of my mum and dad's world, and as people pass through I hope that one of them has the secret to Mia's recovery. Some of them we see almost every day. People like Freya, the "bastard magnet," who cheerfully breezes through the house, chatting to Mia as if nothing's wrong. I like it when Freya comes over. It reminds me of old times, when she and Mia would almost be speaking over each other to get a word in. Sometimes Freya takes her for a drive to get her out of the house and I find myself waiting for a miracle, like them walking through the front door, laughing hysterically over some story Freya has told. But it's only Freya's voice I hear each time and she and I will exchange looks and sometimes there are tears in her eyes because I know that she needs Mia to come back as well.

This is my theory. Mia's not going to go out into her world, so I decide that I need to bring her world to her. She has so many people in her life and I don't know where to start: school, university, work, family friends, colleagues, past teachers, past students. I begin with the people she works with, the ones my dad doesn't relate to.

Sometimes she used to fight with him about them because, as independent as she is, when she went out she wanted my dad and her to be together.

"Go out with them on your own. I'll look after the kids," he'd argue.

"That's a cop-out," she'd say. "I go out with your friends."

"Because my friends are our friends."

"Mine could be ours if you gave them a chance."

"I have given them a chance. I don't watch enough public television and foreign films for them, and all they talk to me about is soccer and the Cosa Nostra." He'd adopt an appalling polished Australian accent, and even Mia would fight hard not to laugh at that. He'd grab her mouth with his hand, making a smile out of it.

"Can we have a maturity moment?" she'd say. "Every time I go to one of these things, I feel like a widow, Rob."

"That's probably because I feel dead when I'm around them."

They're weird, in a way. Sometimes I used to hear them at night and they'd be killing themselves laughing after having a heated argument over dinner. Most of all, she'd be sounding him out. He knows her department by heart. He knows who's lazy, and the strengths and weaknesses of every student in her tutorials. Sometimes we'd be out in Norton Street and bump into one of her students and he'd say, "Oh yeah, Katrina Griffiths, who wrote the paper on McDonald's imperialism." Or else at night they'd talk about what he was working on—the Pirelli house or the Jameson carport. They'd debate about whether he should hire someone else, and they'd talk about going overseas.

"I can't leave my mother," she'd say. "They won't give me time off work. Frankie just started Year Eleven."

"There'll always be an excuse not to relax, Mia."

"It'll cost us at least ten thousand in airfares alone."

"We'll leave the kids with my mother."

Thanks, Dad.

"No way. I couldn't do that."

Mia hated being separated from us.

"Luca would be fine but Frankie would never cope," she'd add.

Thanks, Mum.

My dad liked doing things with her on their own, whereas Mia always had an entourage. Luca, me, Angelina when she was growing up, my nonna now that Nonno's dead, my aunt, Mia's friend from the university who couldn't cope with a breakup. Mia was the mother hen, taking in the problems and issues of all around her.

I'd hear her and her friends talk about men. Freya, the "bastard magnet," would talk about her relationship with her current bastard. "I tell him my problems and he thinks he has to solve them," Freya would say, "when all I want to do is verbalize how I'm feeling."

"Robert doesn't try to solve things," Mia would tell them. "He just tells me, 'Everything's going to be fine.'" She'd say it almost critically, and I couldn't understand why. It'd make me angry. As if she'd have to find something negative just to fit in with the whining.

Telling Mia's world about what's happening isn't easy. They either don't get it or don't want to. Maybe I'm just not selling it well.

"Mia's depressed," I say.

"Tell me about it. I can't get through this work and the department expects miracles." (The any-problem-you-have-mine's-bigger work colleague.)

"Mia's depressed," I tell the next one.

"Nothing to worry about. She'll snap out of it. You know Mia.

Thrives on drama. Tell her to ring me." (The practical university friend who thinks you should be able to juggle everything and not complain.)

"Mia's depressed."

"Well, I can't say I blame her, Francesca. She does everything around there." (Another of Mia's work colleagues. Hates my father.)

"Mia's depressed."

"That's what happens when you take on too much." (Mia's school friend. Gloating voice—a "you sucker" to women who take on heaps and try to have it all. Crucify them! Crucify them!)

Some promise me the moon, others nothing. But by the time I get off the phone, I feel a hundred years old.

Chapter 16

I GET STUCK with Thomas Mackee one afternoon at the bus stop. Luca's at choir practice, and the girls have got various commitments. We stand alongside each other in silence for a while. Then our bus comes along and the psychotic bus driver chooses not to stop for us and we exchange glances. Suddenly we can't pretend the other is not there.

"Why did you ask me to dance in drama?" I ask him.

He rolls his eyes. He does it exaggeratedly and I regret the question.

"Before your feelings get out of hand," he tells me, "I have to warn you that you're not my type."

This time I roll my eyes.

"It was like you were asking me to," he says. "Anyway, I felt like a bloody idiot out there on my own and I thought, who do I want to drag down with me?"

"So why drag me down?"

"Why did you say yes?" he asks.

"You made me laugh and I haven't laughed for, like, ages."

"Because you're a grinner," he confirms.

"Am I?"

"Yep. Not often, but once in a while you have this goofy grin," he tells me. "Most chicks have great smiles, even Finke has a killer of a smile when she forces herself, but you have a goofy grin. See, you're doing the goofy grin now."

I try hard not to, but the more I try the goofier it feels.

"It's not the way to go if you're trying to attract a guy," he advises me, but he's not taking himself seriously and he makes me laugh.

For a moment I can't help thinking how decent he is—that there's some hope for him beyond the obnoxious image he displays. Maybe deep down he is a sensitive guy, who sees us as real people with real issues. I want to say something nice. Some kind of thanks. I stand there, rehearsing it in my mind.

"Oh my God," he says, "did you see that girl's tits?"

Maybe not today.

One of Mia's colleagues comes and visits, and they're in her room for hours. Sue is the head of Mia's department at the university and kind of scares the hell out of us all. Like with my dad, Mia has this way of making people want to hog her, and I always feel that in the eyes of her colleagues, Luca and I are like the enemy who take up too much of her time.

Afterward, I make Sue tea and she talks to me as if I'm an adult and I want to tell her that I'm not.

"Why hasn't she seen a doctor yet?" she asks almost reprimandingly.

"She has. At the very beginning."

"Has she gone back?"

"My dad says they'll only put her on antidepressants."

"Your father doesn't wake up in the morning and see the world through gray-colored glasses. Antidepressants aren't the only answer, but they'll get her on her feet, and from there, she has to take over."

"She doesn't even take Tylenol," I begin.

"And I saw the plate of food you had in there for her," she continues, as if I haven't spoken. "You don't give a starving person a feast. It'll kill her. Begin simply."

I know she's trying to be kind, but Sue is practical. She treats everyone like an adult, except for my father, who she treats like a child.

"Has she lost her job?" I ask.

"No. But her job is the last thing on her mind."

"Is it because of Luca and me . . ."

"You and your brother have to stop thinking she's there to be everything to you."

We're her children, I want to say. *That's what children do, isn't it?*

But I can't imagine Sue's children being like that. She taught them independence, and now they're living in London and Toronto. Mia couldn't even cope with me living in the next suburb with my grandmother.

The next day, when I get home from school, I tap on the door and let myself in. I bring in chamomile tea and toast, and for a moment or two I potter around her. One day I'd like to understand this thing, this ugly sickness that's been sleeping inside of her like a cancer. I wonder if it's sleeping inside of me. I wonder if it was in her when she was sixteen, or if it appeared much later. Looking at it from a distance makes me hate her for being weak. Up close, I've never loved her so much in my life.

I lie alongside her on the bed, where papers brought by Sue, the day before, are scattered all over the place.

"Have you done your homework?" she asks, because I think it's the easiest question for her.

"Most of it. Have you done yours?"

She gives a little sound, like a laugh.

"I'll do it for you," I say. "You used to let me mark your multiple choice stuff."

"That was when I taught Year Eight. It's different."

She hardly has the energy to speak, but I think she wants the company. The contact with the outside world, without having to involve herself in it.

We lie there for a moment in silence.

"Was Sebastian's a mistake?" she asks me quietly.

I don't know how to answer that. I thought I knew the answer, but now it's not so easy to say. So I tell her about the Sebastian girls, and by the time I've spoken for an hour I realize that I can't work them out. Why does Siobhan Sullivan hang out with us, when she's accepted by so many other groups? Any day now she's going to point out how uncool we are and move on. And Tara Finke? The guys in the social justice group hang around her like flies, and as gracious as she is with them, as passionate as they allow her to be without laughing at her like we do sometimes, she's always back with us, arguing, bitching, yelling. It's weird, but I think we're kind of a legitimate group.

I know that Mia thinks that as well, because she nods. In the past, I'd lie on her bed and *her* voice would soothe me. Now it seems like the other way around.

And then I tell her about Will Trombal and about dancing in drama and Shaheen from biology and Eva from economics and Ryan from English and Will Trombal. I tell her about the pathetic Brolin and the lovely Brother Louis and the harassed but kind Ms. Quinn and Will Trombal.

And when I finish speaking, I kiss her cheek and I take away the tray.

And it's empty.

That's how we begin.

Chapter 17

ON THE WAY to the bus stop from school, we walk past this young homeless guy sitting outside a major department store with a cardboard sign saying, *I'm Hungry. Please Feed Me.* Brian Turner from legal studies yells out, "Get a job," and Siobhan laughs and Tara goes on about it all the way to the bus stop.

By the time we sit in the back row of the bus, she and Siobhan have had an argument about it, and the four of us sit in silence. Thomas Mackee is with us as well, because there's nowhere else for him to sit.

The girl in front of us, who hasn't shut up the whole time, stands up and waves to her friends as she gets off the bus.

"I love youse."

We exchange glances.

"What a loser," Siobhan snickers.

"Why is it that someone like Turner who calls out to a beggar on a street isn't a loser, but someone who says 'youse' is?" Tara Finke asks, starting up again.

"Because I think that people should learn how to speak the English language."

"But it's okay for them to be immoral," I say.

"Who's immoral?" Siobhan argues.

"Brian Turner," Tara Finke interrupts. "But it's okay to laugh at his feeble attention seeking, but not to be touched by some nice person who says *youse*."

"How do we know she's nice? Because she expressed her love to her friends?"

"You're judging her by her literacy," Tara says. "You're a literacist."

"You've made that up."

Thomas Mackee packs up his stuff and stands up. "You chicks give me the shits," he says.

"You, on the other hand, brighten up our day," I tell him. "We all regard you as a god."

"You know what we call you? Bitch Spice, Butch Spice, Slut Spice, and Stupid Spice."

He walks away, and we go back to saying nothing for a moment until Justine Kalinsky looks at me and holds out her arms. "My brother reckons that my arms are like Polish salami," she tells me. "Do you think I'm Butch Spice?"

I look at her arms and shake my head.

"Well, I'm a size eight, so I can't possibly be," Siobhan tells us.

"And you're a slut," Tara Finke says matter-of-factly, "so it's quite clear which one you are."

We can't let it go. We get off at Justine Kalinsky's stop just to debate it all the way home.

"I think I could be Butch Spice," Tara tells us. "I've got short hair and that's how those morons think."

"But I've got the stocky build," Justine says. "It's an Eastern European peasant thing."

"No, it's Tara," Siobhan says. "I'm sure of it."

"So between you and me," I tell Justine on the phone that night, "we're either bitchy or stupid."

"Oh God," she moans. "Everyone thinks I'm an idiot."

"Thanks!"

"There is some possible overlap here," Tara explains the next day as we sit in homeroom. "I think Francesca could be Bitch Spice, but some people do think she's stupid as well."

"I kissed two guys one night in Year Nine, so I could be Slut Spice too," I tell them.

"No. Not possible. Because what would that make me? I'm not stupid, nor am I bitchy," Siobhan says.

"Siobhan, you're the whole spice rack as far as some people are concerned," Tara informs her.

"Would you consider me bitchy, stupid, slutty, or butch?" I ask Shaheen in biology.

"The obvious one," he says, knowing exactly what I'm talking about, which worries me. "By the way, is it true that you and Trombal pashed?"

"He was drunk."

"You should go out with wogs."

"He is a wog."

"But not like us."

"Are you asking me out, Shaheen?"

"Are you sick? As if you're my type. You didn't even know who Tupac was."

I try not to look offended. "You could have let me down a lot more gently."

He laughs. "You're cool. Even though you're not a Leb."

"It's obvious which one you are," Jimmy Hailler tells me as we walk through Hyde Park.

"If it's so obvious, why can't I see it?"

"Because you live in your own world and can't see anything."

"Then which one am I?"

"You're all four. You're constantly bitching about things under your breath; you come across bloody stupid because you don't speak; on a particular angle in that uniform on an overcast day with your hair up, you've got that stocky butch thing happening; plus you're pashing other girls' boyfriends, which makes you a slut."

"Thank you for feeding my paranoia."

"No prob. Want to hang out at your place?" he says as we reach the bus stop.

"No."

"See. There's the bitch coming through."

The bus stops in front of us. "Get stuffed."

I get on and show my pass.

"I've got nowhere else to go," he cries in exaggerated anguish. "I've-

got-nowhere-else-to-go," he blubbers dramatically in a pathetic broken voice, clutching the pole.

The bus driver and I exchange looks and I roll my eyes.

"*An Officer and a Gentleman,*" I tell the driver. "You know? Richard Gere?"

"First sign of trouble and you're both off."

We get to Annandale and he takes out a cigarette and offers one to me.

"I try not to indulge. It's a filthy habit," I tell him.

"I love that word *filthy*. I love the way you force it out of your mouth like it's some kind of vermin you want to get rid of."

"You've had vermin in your mouth?"

"You're mean in that way, you know. You don't let anyone get away with pathetic analogies."

When we arrive at my house, I look over at the people across the road.

"Those people have no life," I tell him.

"They look happy, though."

He gives them a wave and they wave back.

We walk inside and I put on the teakettle, throw my bag into my bedroom, and push him toward the living room.

"Sit down and don't touch anything," I tell him before walking into Mia's study. Today she's sitting on the couch, in her nightgown as usual, her laptop in front of her, staring into space. She doesn't want to lose the conferences and is making an attempt at writing the paper.

"I'm making some tea," I say, kissing her. "I'll bring it in a min—"

"Hi."

I turn around and Jimmy's at the study door.

Mia looks at me curiously.

"James Hailler," he says, walking over to the couch and extending his hand for her to shake.

I'm furious, but he ignores me. My mum shakes his hand.

"What are you doing?" he asks her.

"Trying to write a paper."

I look at him and indicate the door with my eyes. He reminds me of our dog. He totally ignores any look that demands obedience. Instead, he sits on the couch.

"What's it on?"

"The role of fantasy in popular culture."

"I'm your man. It's my genre."

I hear the kettle whistling and I ignore it. He looks at me and indicates the door with his eyes.

"The kettle," he reminds me. "I like mine with a squeeze of lemon."

I'm reluctant to leave him in there. Just say he asks her why she's in her nightgown? Just say he spreads it around the school? I don't know this guy. All I know is that he looks like he's here to stay.

"And get James some biscuits, Frankie," my mum says.

I prepare the tea and make my mum a salad sandwich, straining my ears to hear what they're talking about. I don't hear my dad walk in, but I see him as I come out of the kitchen into the corridor. He's standing at the study door, and I come up behind him and give him a gentle push out of the way.

"This is Jimmy, Papa. Jimmy, my dad."

"I didn't catch your name," Jimmy says to my dad, getting off the couch and extending a hand.

"Mr. Spinelli," my dad says a bit coldly.

"It's Robert." This comes from my mum as I place the tray next to her.

Jimmy makes himself comfortable on the couch again and serves her the tea before biting into a biscuit.

"Hmm. What's for dinner?"

When he leaves, my father comes into my room.

"He's a drug user. I can tell."

"How?"

"I know about marijuana, you know."

"It's called pot."

"Oh, aren't we the smarty-pants."

"I think you mean 'smart-ass.' "

"I don't need this right now, Frankie. I've got enough things to fix up around here."

"If you don't want me to hang out with potheads, you should have sent me to Pius."

I feel as if I'm doing Jimmy Hailler a disservice because he's probably not a pothead, but it's a way to rile my dad up. I'm not sure why I want to do that, but I just do.

He doesn't say anything else. Later, I hear him in Luca's bedroom, doing his quality-time thing. But I know he's dying to get into that room to be with Mia while we have to watch it all from a distance. And I hate that distance. Because from a distance, Luca and I see it blurred. And blurred, it looks worse than anyone can ever imagine.

Chapter 18

THE MORNING BUS trips to school are a combination of Thomas Mackee's music, Tara Finke's protest, and Justine's mooning over Tuba Guy.

Sometimes Thomas Mackee will stick an earphone into my ear and ask me to listen to a song. When I get over the revulsion of putting something in my ear that's been in his, I sit back and let the music take over, and for a half hour there's something comforting about someone's heart beating at the same rhythm as mine.

Other times, I sit back and listen to Tara organize the troops. If it's not a food drive outside school, where most of the homeless hang out at night, it's volunteering for a social justice day run by the Education Office or organizing a protest outside a local MP's office, who she feels is doing nothing about the detainment of refugees.

A stubborn part of me doesn't want to get involved. Mia spent the last four years asking why I couldn't be "like that Tara Finke girl." "Because I want to have friends," I'd tell her.

"Some of those people won't even know what the issue's about," I say to Tara Finke. "They protest for the sake of protest."

"That's a cop-out and you know it," Tara says.

"Are you denying it?" I ask.

"No. But it's like the argument 'don't donate to third-world countries because the money mightn't get to them.' People only say that because it makes them feel better about the fact that they do nothing."

Thomas Mackee is sitting next to us listening to his Discman. Tara takes one of the earphones out of his ear.

"You're coming with us," she says firmly.

"I don't think so," he says, knowing exactly what she's referring to, as if he's listened to our conversation.

"Don't pretend for one moment that we haven't caught on that you've got a social conscience," she accuses.

"Not listening," he singsongs.

"Yes, you are listening."

He turns off the Discman, takes out the other earphone, and stares at her coldly. "*No,* I'm *not* listening." He points to himself. "My world." And then he points to her. "Your world. Different worlds."

"Where's your world now, Mackee?" she asks. "Where are they after school when you're hanging out with us?"

"I don't hang out with you. I take the bus home with you. Get the difference. I'm not into protesting. I don't want to save the world. I don't care about anything, and I don't care that I don't care."

Tara stares at him and then nods. "I'm sorry," she says honestly.

Thomas Mackee looks surprised for a moment, and then he nods back, as if he accepts the apology.

"It's a habit of mine to force people into things," she adds meekly.

"T'sokay."

Oh God, Thomas Mackee, don't fall for this.

"You could get into trouble at school, and where would that get you?" she continues. "I mean, you're thinking of joining a punk band one day, right? And what if they ever found out that you protested about something? It'd ruin your reputation. As a punk artist you need a squeaky-clean image, not a rebellious one."

He stops nodding when he works out where she's going with this. He has that stupid look on his face. His "Huh?" look.

"What are you looking at?" he asks Luca gruffly.

Luca giggles. He has that Year-Five-need-to-get-attention-of-senior-boys thing happening. Sometimes, Thomas Mackee carries Luca to school, holding him upside down by just one leg, and I picture my brother's head splattered all over Market Street, but I don't stop him. If Luca is killing himself laughing, I don't have the heart to stop anything.

And slowly the mornings begin to change. Nothing too friendly or exciting, but by the time I get to school, the sick feeling that I wake up with every morning disappears. Not for long, but enough to get me through the day.

Chapter 19

WE GET INVITED to another party. It's a Year Eleven guy, but most of the Year Twelves are invited as well, and I wonder if Will Trombal will be there.

My dad drops us off at the same time that Thomas Mackee drives his friends in. He does an exaggerated double take when he sees us and, as usual, his friends kill themselves laughing as if it's the most hysterical thing they've ever seen.

Jimmy Hailler is swinging his legs from the front porch, smoking a joint. He beckons me over and pats the space next to him.

"It's nerdsville inside," he informs me.

Someone puts on an Abba CD, and I hear a combination of cheers and boos.

Jimmy offers me his joint. "You might need this to get through 'Dancing Queen.'"

I decline with a laugh. "Dance with me."

"Only losers dance to this type of music."

* * *

I dance with Tara and Justine, squashed on the tiny living room dance floor with the jaded and the cool and the clever and the straightie-one-eighties, as Jimmy Hailler would call us. But Abba has the ability to unite the masses and it goes from there. At the part where Agnetha and Frida sing "Dig in the Dancing Queen," Justine does a digging motion and actually starts a trend, which is frightening. At one stage I'm doing *Saturday Night Fever* dance steps with Shaheen. It's like I'm high on Jimmy Hailler's joint without having smoked it. As usual, there's heaps of drinking, and combined with junk food, my stomach feels like it's going to revolt. But it's fun, and Mia being sick belongs to another world.

I finish dancing and I see Will Trombal looking at me. He's indulged in the hair gel, and in surf-shop streetwear he looks impressive. But it's the look in his eyes that I can't help responding to, and I think to myself, forget the girlfriend. Just go for it. And I want to. But his girlfriend is there, a smiler, not a grinner.

Later on, I get some air. Jimmy is playing knuckle thumping with some guy, and they're both killing themselves laughing because they keep on missing.

I sense someone beside me and I know it's Will Trombal. We look at each other and don't say a word for a moment or two.

"Are you okay?" he asks.

"Do I not look okay?"

"You look great."

We do the nodding thing, but I don't look away. I think our fingers even brush up against each other. Something light and static.

"Is that your girlfriend with you?"

He nods. "Veronica."

Thomas Mackee sticks his head between us and makes kissing sounds, just as Justine comes outside and pulls me away.

"It's Siobhan," she says, somewhat distressed.

I follow her into the house and I see Tara standing in front of a door, her arms folded, a don't-mess-with-me look on her face.

I go into the room and come face-to-face with this guy called Tim Lang. Siobhan's bad taste in guys never ceases to amaze me. For a moment, I don't let him pass. I just stare at him, and then he pushes past me.

"Lesbians," he says snidely to Tara.

"Oh, very original," Tara says.

Siobhan is sitting on a bed, half-naked, crying hysterically, mascara running down her face.

I bend down to button up her shirt, a bit embarrassed because it's not as if I've ever seen her half-naked.

She slaps my hand away.

I pull her into the adjoining bathroom and stick her face into the sink, and she fights me hard. There are mascara streaks all down her face. Outside, I hear "Endless Love" and I think of Will Trombal dancing with his girlfriend.

I dunk her face in the water again.

"If your father sees you like this, he'll kill you."

"What do you care? What do you care about anything?"

She makes a retching sound that I've become very familiar with, and I pull her toward the toilet, where she vomits. I find it hard not to vomit myself, but she's crying and I hold her forehead the way Mia used to hold mine and I feel so lonely and I want my mother. Suddenly, I'm crying too.

I wipe her face and I finish buttoning up her shirt. She's looking at me, a little stunned. My eyes feel swollen and my face grimy, and I must look worse than her at the moment.

"You used to be my best friend," she whispers. "Do you remember?"

"I don't know who I was," I whisper back.

We walk out of the room calmly. Some of the guys are snickering, but thankfully everyone is belting out "Summer Nights," outdoing each other as best they can.

Tara is speaking to Ryan Burke and some of the social justice guys.

"We're going," I tell her.

I grab Thomas Mackee as we walk out.

"We need your car."

For a moment he looks torn between his friends and us. Then Tara says, "Thomas, are you with us?"

And for once, he doesn't say a word.

At midnight, we take turns running around Hyde Park sobering Siobhan up. It's freezing cold, and those of us who aren't running are huddled on the grass together, looking at the stars.

"It was a crap party anyway," Thomas says. "Do you want to know my theory?" he rabbits on. "Retro is going to be the downfall of the twenty-first century."

"What happened in there?" Justine asks me quietly. I think she's talking about me, rather than Siobhan. I haven't said a word since the party.

"He called her something she's not," I say quietly. It's the first thing I've said since the party. Tara comes back with Siobhan just as I say it and we stand huddled against each other and I feel Siobhan's hand come across my back. It feels warm.

And in the dark silence it makes me feel strong.

"My mother's had a nervous breakdown. She's suffering from depression and she won't get out of the house. And every day it's killing us more."

I can't believe I've said it out loud. The truth doesn't set you free, you know. It makes you feel awkward and embarrassed and defenseless and red in the face and horrified and petrified and vulnerable. But free? I don't feel free. I feel like shit.

No one says anything. Because there's nothing really to say.

But then I feel Justine Kalinsky take my hand, and I feel Siobhan's shock and Tara Finke's empathy.

"Don't tell Will Trombal," Thomas Mackee says. "He'll probably try and comfort you, and tonight when he was speaking to you, he got a hard-on."

The others are disgusted, their voices all mingling into one.

"You're such a dickhead!"

"Why can't you act human?"

"You are so insensitive."

"You've made her cry, you asshole. She's shaking."

But I'm shaking because I'm laughing so much. I'm laughing so much that I have tears streaming down my face and then I'm sobbing until it's like I'm going to choke and I'm feeling so many things that I don't think my mind can handle it. I can hardly breathe and it must sound so frightening that Thomas Mackee grabs me and holds me and everyone's saying, "It's okay, Francesca, it's okay, Francesca," and they're crying too.

We stay like that for a while. No one tries to analyze it or offer solutions. No one interrupts. Sometimes, momentarily, I'm embarrassed by the whole disclosure, but I realize that I trust these people and I don't know how or when that happened.

Later on, we walk back to Thomas Mackee's car and I ask him why he doesn't drink.

"Because I want to be the first male in the Mackee family to reach forty and still have his liver," he says bluntly.

In the dark I can't tell whether he's serious or not.

I lean against a streetlight and throw up, just near his shoe. He looks down at the ground and then at me.

"The guacamole was a mistake," he says matter-of-factly.

For the second time that night he makes me laugh. "Don't make me have to like you," I tell him.

Chapter 20

IT'S THE END of the term, and instead of feeling excited, I'm depressed. The thought of two weeks in the house with my mum in the state she's in is unbearable. Worse still, I'm frightened that any type of progress I've made with people at school will be lost over school break. The foundations of our friendships are too weak, and I'm not sure if they will hold.

I ring up my Stella friends, one by one. I haven't heard from them since the time on the bus with Tina, so I figure it's about time I made an attempt.

I get invited to a Pius party, but all I want, really, is to see them on their own. The way it used to be.

A part of me itches to ring up Justine Kalinsky and the girls, but I don't. I'm scared they'll say "Who?" when I tell them it's me, and I know they'll probably have a hundred other things to do. But I have nothing. Just Luca, and even he's too busy for me.

On the weekend, I have a dress fitting with Angelina and the bridesmaids. One's her best friend from college, and the other is her cousin Vera from her mother's side, who my aunt insisted on.

For someone who's never sewn in her life, Angelina has done a brilliant job. She's got enough taste to be able to pull off something extraordinary, but the dresses are low-cut and I can't help looking down at my cleavage at least every five seconds.

"You look great," Angelina reassures me. "Just don't think about it."

"It's in my face, Angelina. I don't have a choice."

"You should be proud of it. You could be like Vera, who has nothing."

Vera is obsessed with dieting and the gym and has lost any body fat she ever possessed.

"Thanks, Angelina," Vera says dryly, adjusting her push-up bra.

Later on, Angelina and the bridesmaids take me up to Haberfield for coffee and ricotta cannoli.

"How's Mia?" she asks.

I shrug.

"Don't let her get comfortable with this, Francesca," Vera says, as if the whole world knows about it. "Robert's a good-looking guy and he'll get sick of—"

"Vera, shut up," Angelina tells her.

"What do you mean?" I ask.

"She means she's an idiot and she doesn't know Uncle Robert."

"Men don't hang around depressed women forever. They get sick of it. They need to have sex," Vera continues.

Angelina stands up and takes me by the arm.

"I'm going outside for a ciggy."

My head is spinning.

"She's an ignoramus, like everyone on my mother's side of the family," she tells me outside.

"Are people saying that my father is going to leave my mother?"

"They're jealous, so they're going to go around putting the *malocchio* on it," she says, referring to the evil eye.

"Just say my mum stays like this forever? Like Zia Annunziata in Sicily, who hasn't said a word for forty-five years."

"Says who? Nonna? Would you speak to Nonna if she nicked off with your fiancé?"

"Nonno was engaged to Annunziata?"

"Uh-huh. And the flirty younger sister, Nonna, stows away on the boat with him coming out here. He was supposed to bring Zia over when he arrived, but then he had to marry Nonna."

"Wow."

"Plus she nicked off with Zia's S biscuit recipe."

"Oh my God!"

Angelina nods.

"That town in Sicily was like *Melrose Place* and Nonna was Heather Locklear."

She puts out the cigarette. "Don't listen to Vera. She's got as much intelligence as those dumbbells she holds on her power walks."

"I just want it to go back to the way it was."

"It'll never go back to the way it was, Frankie. But you have to make sure it goes forward."

She drops me off and I go straight to my mum's room. My dad's in there with her, holding her. She's asleep and he's kissing her cheek.

"She doesn't want to have sex!" I yell. "She's sick."

He looks at me in shock.

"Frankie, what's got into you?"

I storm into my room and slam the door, furious at him for allowing people to make up rumors. I ring up Michaela from Stella's and I ask her if she'd like to do something. I try to remember what made our relationship work in the past. Was it because she had a sense of humor and treated me well? And if it was because of that, why did I feel so grateful that people treated me well?

But Michaela can't do anything tonight. She's having a sleepover at Natalia's. I want to invite myself over, but I keep on thinking she'll invite me instead.

But she doesn't.

So I ring Justine Kalinsky and I say, "It's Francesca Spinelli," and she says, "Francesca, you've got to stop using last names. How are you doing?" and I say, "I feel like shit," and I don't know how it happens, but by eight o'clock that night I'm lying next to her on the couch with Siobhan and Tara and we're eating junk food and watching a Keanu movie.

And I want to stay on that couch for the rest of my life.

Chapter 21

WE START TERM three with a House meeting, and I get to look at
Will Trombal for a whole twenty minutes while he speaks. He is a
man of minimal words, Will is. His stares are long, his pauses never-
ending, and he always thinks before he speaks. He has a quiet
confidence devoid of the ego, and earnestness and sincerity I find
confronting to witness. When the meeting is over, as I'm jostling
out of the foyer, I feel someone grab my arm from behind and he's
there, facing me, an irritated look on his face.

"What?" he says.

We're pushed and shoved, but I don't mind the contact.

"What what?"

"Why did you roll your eyes?"

"I didn't," I lie.

"Every time I spoke, you rolled your eyes," he accuses.

"Then don't look at me when you speak."

"If I want to look at you, I'll look at you."

"Will, this conversation is ridiculous. Now, I'm an expert on ridiculous conversations, but you're way out of your element, which means that I'll win. And going by the Tolstoy/Trotsky thing, I don't think you'll cope very well with your loss."

He looks at me for a moment, and then he seems to relax and that half smile kind of appears.

"So, how was your break?" he asks.

"Long. Yours?"

"Confusing." He's looking at me intensely. "I'm a month away from recording my university preferences."

I can tell he's all over the place.

"And I know *exactly* what I'm going to write down," he continues, as if I've responded, "and that frightens the hell out of me."

"Do you know what my theory is?" I tell him, although it's really Mia's theory. "Fear's good. It keeps things interesting."

His face softens. "In a good year, you kind of look as if you'd be fearless."

I shake my head. "I haven't had a good year for a while."

Somehow he ends up walking me to class. It's like something out of an American teen flick, and I find myself swinging as I walk alongside him, to music that I can hear in my head. I can't look at him, so I have to rely on every other sense. The smell of his aftershave, the feel of his elbow when we accidentally brush up against each other, the resonance of his gravelly voice.

A great feeling comes over me. Because for a moment, I kind of like who I am.

In drama, we start a Shakespeare unit and Ortley suggests a production for fourth term. *"Henry IV, Part 1,"* he says. "You'll relate to the rebellious son wanting to hang out with his idiot friends at the pub."

I like looking at his face when he speaks. Sometimes he spits, actually he spits all the time, but I think that's passionate. He loves words and he rolls them around in his mouth like a luscious plum, slobbering on the sides, and then he'll use his hands, touching his mouth as if he's taking the words out and throwing them to us.

And boy do we flinch. He uses swear words in class, not at us, but about the texts, and it kind of excites us because here's a man who's not scared of talking about sex and passion. It's weird, because he's about fifty and has the craggiest face and the most demented stares, but in his classes I feel tapped into something, a kind of attraction.

"Wouldn't it be hard to be rebellious and cool with a name like Henry?" Thomas asks.

"Hal, to his friends."

The bell rings and we stream out. I'm unimpressed by the choice of play, but I don't say anything.

"Francesca?"

"Yes." I walk to Ortley's desk.

"You rolled your eyes."

Oh God, another one. "It's a condition I have," I lie, because it's quicker than explaining.

"I'm interested in what you think."

"About the production?"

"Of course."

I've taken a truth serum. It got a smile out of Will, so I give it a go, sitting down in front of him.

145

"*Henry IV* has only one good female role. Kate. The Welsh girl can't speak English. So it's pretty limited. I think we should do a Shakespeare with more chicks in it."

He's taken aback, and then he laughs. "You look better than last term. Are you okay?" It's a gruff query.

I don't know how to deal with this question. When it's not asked, I hate everyone, but when Justine asks me and when Mr. Ortley demands to know, it's hard. I haven't practiced the right polite answer. It's only the first day back and he's put me on the spot.

"Some days are good and other days are shockers," I say, because the truth serum hasn't worn off yet.

He looks at me and nods. "Same here."

I can't help grinning.

"Can you act?" he asks.

"I was in *Oliver* in Year Six."

"Nancy?"

"Fagin."

He's impressed.

"How about *Macbeth*? Do you know your Shakespeare?"

"*Macbeth*, yes. I'm not of woman born, you know," I say, referring to the fact that the witches predict that Macbeth will be killed by someone not of woman born, who ends up being someone born by Cesarean section birth. "When I went to see a production in Year Nine, I thought I was a freak because of it."

"Why? The freak ends up killing the monster, doesn't he?"

"Yeah, I guess so."

He stands up and picks up his stuff. "Let me think about the change of play," he says. "But remember, I've got a reputation for excellent productions. If you don't wow me in the *Macbeth* auditions, we'll do *Henry IV* and you'll play the Welsh girl who can't speak English."

"Deal."

On the bus I tell Tara about the possible change.

"Macbeth?"

"Uh-huh."

"And you think that's a victory?"

"Why, isn't it?"

"Think of the women. Three witches, one bitch, and one submissive housewife."

"I wouldn't call Lady Macduff a submissive housewife," I argue.

"She's a nag. She nags Macduff to death," Thomas tells us, pulling an earphone out of his head.

"I think she's feisty," Justine says.

"And she still dies," Tara informs me. "Lady Macbeth kills herself, the witches disappear. Notice we become redundant in all the victory."

"It's just a play," I say, irritated.

"No it's not. It's an exposé of how strong-minded women end up either going insane or being clobbered."

"Or described as chicks with beards," Thomas says.

"Huh?" Siobhan asks.

"He's talking about the witches," I explain. "And let's not forget that the 'strong-minded' Lady Macbeth was a psycho bitch from hell."

"This is not good," Tara says, shaking her head.

"I disagree," Justine argues. "I think they're finally listening to us."

"I would have preferred the one about the guy hanging out with his friends in the pub," Thomas says.

147

"I'm going to go for Lady Macbeth," I tell them, "and worse still, I've decided my audition piece will be the one where she says, 'Unsex me now,' which is going to be hard in front of a bunch of morons."

Thomas is finally interested.

"Sex?"

"No sex," Tara explains. "She's saying, get the woman out of me and let the guy part take over because only guys can do disgusting, revolting, shitty things."

"Woman, you're a worry," he mutters under his breath.

My dad and I walk home from grocery shopping in Johnston Street. We pass the kids at the top of the street who have built their own grind pole and are flying in the air and landing in the middle of the road.

"Get off the road," my father says as we pass them.

He's in his flip-flops and work clothes and the kids snicker, but I give them the evil eye.

Sometimes I look at Dad and think he seems so sad that he might burst. Mia has been the love of his life since they were fifteen, and I think his whole identity has been wrapped up in her.

"What do you talk about at night?" I ask him.

He thinks for a moment.

"I do the talking, which is funny, isn't it?"

Mia's argument had always been that my father doesn't talk enough about what's going on inside his head. She comes from the school of getting it out of your system, whereas he comes from the school of stewing over it.

"It's not like there's an answer or just one reason," he tells me.

"Are you saying there's more than one reason?"

"I'm just saying that I wish I could say it was this or that."

"I wish you'd tell us at least what one of the thises and thats is!"

I don't recognize who I am with my father these days. Lately, when I speak to him there's this bite in my tone and I can't stop it and I don't know why. Do I blame him for all this, because Mia seems too fragile to blame?

"She was just tired from a lot of things," he explains. "Maybe she needed a break and she just didn't let us know."

"Once, at the beginning of last year, she told me that she wanted to stay home and not work, and she was so happy about it," I say. And I don't know where that comes from. Where have I hidden that memory?

He stops for a moment, and I can see something change on his face.

"Did she ever say that to you?" I ask him, trying to recall the conversation I once had with her.

"I don't remember."

"She was ecstatic about it. That I can remember. Do you remember?"

He shakes his head and begins walking again.

"After Nonno died," I press on, because somehow memories come floating back in bits and pieces, "for so long she was sad, and then one day I remember that she was happy. But then it changed again. Maybe it was something I did. Or with Mummy and me, it was probably something I didn't do."

"You and Mia are just like Mia and her mother were."

In the distance, I see Jimmy Hailler talking to the people across the road. They know more about him than me.

"Doesn't he have a home to go to?"

"I have no idea."

"I don't want him in your bedroom."

"Papa! Don't be so old-fashioned. We're just friends."

"And look at his pants. Why doesn't he just wear them around his ankles?"

"Look at yourself. You look like something out of a yobbo retrospective."

"Who teaches you these words?" he asks in mock anguish. It's the first time I've heard him joke around for a while, and it makes my heart sing.

We approach the house and I wave at Jimmy.

"And if he thinks he's eating with us, he's got another thing coming," my dad says.

Jimmy approaches us and takes the shopping bags from me, looking inside them.

"Lamb roast. Am I invited?"

Chapter 22

IN LEGAL STUDIES we're in the library, researching stuff on the Internet. Thomas is sitting next to me, with his earphones discreetly plugged into the computer, tapping away and nodding his head. Once in a while he breaks into song, off-key, and it's hard to concentrate. I find myself typing in the word "depression." There are thousands of entries, and I'm stunned by the amount of information.

"What are you doing?" I hear Justine ask.

I quickly switch off the monitor, but she reaches over and switches it back on.

I don't know why I ever thought Justine was shy. Sometimes I try hard to remember her at Stella's, but the Justine of St. Stella's is a blur, some kind of wallpaper print that no one actually took any notice of. Here, since it's a musical school, they love the whole accordion thing. Her nerdiness kind of makes her cool. "She kills me," Eva Rodriguez says. I don't know when Justine's giggles stopped getting on my nerves, but we've fallen into this habit of talking online every night, mostly about Tuba Guy and Will and music. Weirdly enough, her taste is similar to Thomas Mackee's: new-age punk, alternative stuff, and show tunes. They are passionate about the local music scene and burn CDs for each other, having deep-and-meaningfuls about the actual music and lyrics, and somehow I've got used to their tastes. Mine was a combination of everything Mia and my Stella friends listened to, but I kind of like the lack of structure in Justine and Thomas's, even though no one else has ever heard of them.

Today, Justine stands over me, pressing the scroll bar on the computer down.

"You have to narrow it down," she explains. "There's just different types, that's all."

"You're an expert, are you?"

"*Hello.* I'm Polish. My family invented depression."

I feel bad for being so flippant, and she squeezes in next to me as we scroll down.

"Is she delusional? Suffers hallucinations?" she asks, reading off the screen.

"Not that I know of."

"Low mood, lack of enjoyment, and loss of interest in usual pastimes and becoming generally withdrawn?" she continues.

"Yep."

"Downturned mouth, frown lines on her forehead?"

"Uh-huh."

"That could be anyone," Thomas butts in. "I mean, look at Brolin."

"Are we talking to you?" I ask, turning my back on him.

Justine reads down the page. "Okay, if it's acute depression it can last between three and nine months, although it can drag on for years. It says you 'need to address the root cause of the symptoms for it to stop.' "

"I have no idea what the 'root cause of the symptoms' is. What does it suggest that could be?"

"Anything. Marital problems?"

I think for a moment.

"He takes off his socks and leaves them anywhere, and he's happy to go along with anything except sometimes going out with some of her friends, but I don't think that's the issue. I think she's worried that his idea of retiring one day is sitting on the couch with her, which up till this year was totally foreign to her because I'd never seen her sit on a couch for more than five minutes in her whole life. And he can never understand why she has to worry about who they'll be in thirty years' time and not just enjoy who they are now. Plus she does all the running around after us and he says, 'Why? Who's telling you to?' And she says—"

"I've heard my mother say it," Justine interrupts.

"Someone has to," we say, mimicking our mothers. Even Thomas joins in.

"This is a personal conversation," I tell him.

"About where your parents will be in the future? I understand these questions in life. Do you know what I'm listening to right now?" he asks. "It's called 'Ten Years.' Listen to this:

"Will you have played your part?
Will you have carved your mark?"

He looks at me, nodding his head slowly and dramatica

"Where are you this very moment?"

"Sitting next to a dickhead, Thomas. And you?"

"Ignore him," Justine says, continuing to scroll. "How about 'bereavement, losing one's job, financial stress'?"

"Not the last two. But maybe bereavement. She was crazy about my nonno, but when he died she just took over everything because other people were hysterical during that time and she had to take care of everyone. And it was a crazy time for her because she had been offered a lecturing job at the university and she couldn't take time out and go to pieces, you know. She just got on with it. That's what she does . . . or did. She just gets on with things. And Dad, being Dad, would tell her that everything was going to be fine."

"Which is a bit of a lie," Thomas says. "Your no-no was dead and your dad was pretending that he wasn't, which was the last thing your mother needed."

"My nonno, not my no-no. And my father is an optimist. He sees the bright side of things."

"That's called denial," Thomas says knowingly.

"You listen to a few song lyrics and now you're a psychologist?"

"You're like your father. *Denial.*"

"Did I ask for your advice?" I ask him.

"How about alcoholism?" Justine asks. "Excessive consumption of caffeine?"

"I can't put my mother's depression down to too many macchiatos at Bar Italia."

"They've got suggestions to deal with it. Eat wholesome food, spend some time in a stress-free environment with a companion who is willing to listen to you, get plenty of fresh air and sunlight, exercise six days per week, and take plenty of vitamins B and C."

Thomas looks at me and rolls his eyes.

"Obviously these are just simple solutions," Justine adds, realizing how weak it all sounds.

"She can't even get off the couch, Justine, and they advise her to go to a gym?"

"Antidepressants," Thomas suggests. "My father was on them for six months once. Fun times."

My relationship with my father begins to get worse. It's almost as if we're embarking on a custody battle over my mum. Every time I try to press him about what the doctors have to say, he's vague or I feel he's lying.

"Your nonna's doctor said she was stressed," he explains one night while cooking dinner.

"She's not stressed. She's suffering acute depression," I say, liking the way the jargon slips out as if I know what I'm talking about.

My brother is in front of the fridge squeezing Ice Magic on his tongue. I point to Luca, who escapes outside with it.

"I've told you before," he says. "Stop seeing this as something you have to solve. She has a lot on her plate."

"Papa, she won't eat anything off her plate. She needs anti-depressants."

"You don't know what you're talking about."

"Nor do you!"

"I don't want her on antidepressants," he says flatly. "Nonna

Celia was on them for years, and it was a nightmare for Mia growing up that way."

"That was years ago, Papa. Things have changed."

"We can work this out ourselves," he continues, despite the fact that I'm shaking my head.

"No we can't. Papa, it's been three months. It's not going to go away."

"I've spoken about it with her and she doesn't want antidepressants."

"What she wants isn't the issue anymore!" I'm shouting, but I can't help it. "Getting her better is, and she doesn't just belong to you. She belongs to us as well."

"I'm the adult here, Francesca. I make the decisions, not you. You're the kid."

"Oh, *now* I'm the kid. When I have to ring up the university to go into what's wrong with her, I'm an adult, but now I'm a kid because you're the expert."

"Do you think I haven't looked into this?" he asks. "She doesn't have a chemical imbalance. She doesn't need to get addicted to something. She doesn't need tablets giving her nightmares."

"You have no idea what you're talking about. I've done my research too. She needs to get on her feet. She hasn't been outside, on her own, for three months."

"Go do your homework."

"Oh, fantastic argument, Papa. 'Keep the house tidy. Do your homework. Be a good girl.' That's going to fix everything, isn't it? That'd make me want to get out of bed if I were Mummy."

It's total silence after that. The food is cardboard in my mouth, but I race to finish it because I want to get into Mia's room before he does.

Later, I snuggle up beside her. "Tell me the story about when I almost drowned?" I ask her, so then she can be the hero and it'll make her feel better. But she says nothing and I switch on the television and I pretend that what we're watching is funny. It's a sitcom about a family, two kids, a mum, and a dad. Their idea of tension is an argument about who gets the cottage out back. At the end, everyone's happy because that's what happens in television land. Things get solved in thirty minutes.

God, I want to live there.

Chapter 23

MS. QUINN SENDS me up to the counselor on Friday. Sometimes I wonder how I come across to these people. Is it written all over my face, or does the whole world just know every detail of my family life?

I stand in front of Ms. Quinn's desk, unimpressed. I'm not interested in someone picking my brain. Me going to see a counselor is not going to make Mia any better.

"I send everyone up to him," she tells me.

"No you don't."

"How do you know, Francesca? People keep counselor visits quiet, so it's not as if they're going to tell you they've gone to see him."

"I don't feel like talking. I'm fine, anyway. Actually, I'm better than I've ever been, and if I have to speak to anyone, I trust you."

Saying that to teachers always works. The emotional ones like Ms. Quinn thrive on being needed.

She smiles. "I'm glad."

"Thanks for your concern, though," I say, turning to walk out.

"No problem at all. Come and see me after you've spoken to him. I'll ring to tell him you're on your way up."

I turn back to face her.

"I thought we agreed that I wasn't going."

"No," she says, in what I know is feigned confusion. "You go to Mr. Hector and I go on to be the least gullible teacher in this school."

No wonder the guys say she's a bitch.

"Would it hurt to speak to someone who is completely objective?" she asks.

"Objective about what?"

"Objective about what's going on at home, Francesca."

"You don't know anything about what's going on in my home."

"We could do this for another hour, but I've got classes and you're still going to the counselor."

"That's bullying!"

"Oh please, I'm nowhere near the bullying stage."

I face her, arms folded. If this woman thinks she's going to win this one, she's sorely mistaken.

The counselor's not that bad.

Not that I can see myself wanting to visit him again, but he doesn't try to make me write things down or keep a journal of my pain, and he never once tells me that things are going to be fine.

I explain to him that my dad tells me that things are going to be fine all the time. Mr. Hector asks me how I feel about that, and because I sense he's going to start analyzing me, I make it up and tell him what he wants to hear.

That every time my dad says that everything's okay, I want to scream. Because everything's not okay. The woman who has driven this family for longer than I've been alive can't leave the house, so how can that be okay? "Okay" is coming home and your parents are having an argument. "Okay" is Mia picking us up from school and going grocery shopping and us dancing in the aisle to the pathetic music over the PA system. "Okay" is Mia telling me what's best for me and me completely disagreeing, and it's Mia telling my father to carry the load a bit more because she's sick of having to do all the running around. "Okay" is listening to them have sex at night and blocking your ears because you think listening to your parents having sex is a form of child abuse. "Okay" is them bantering with each other in front of you and you not understanding a single word because they're speaking in riddles they alone understand. "Okay" is knowing what to expect.

In the end I don't say much to him at all, and I go back to Ms. Quinn, who's speaking on the phone and eyeing me at the same time. I like her office. It's incredibly tidy, but it's got personality, not to mention a sofa. She has music playing all the time. Today it's Counting Crows, and I feel as melancholy as the lead singer's voice.

"I'm cured," I tell her when she gets off the phone.

"Are you, now?"

"Isn't that what you want to hear?"

"No. I want to hear that you're happy."

"Are *you*?"

She thinks for a moment. She's almost my mother's age, and they're kind of similar in a way. If my mum were well, I could imagine them hitting it off.

"Most of the time I am," she tells me.

"Why not all of the time?"

She eyes me suspiciously. "You're trying to get out of Mr. Brolin's class, aren't you?"

I grin and shrug. "Maybe. I bet if you were in my shoes, you would too, but you're going to plead professionalism and not put down a colleague."

"Go to class."

I kind of like her when she's relaxed. She doesn't have that tired, looking-for-something-better expression some of my Stella teachers had. When I grow up, I think I'm going to be a teacher or maybe even a counselor.

I walk to Brolin's class feeling lighter in mood. He gives me a detention for being late without a note. Actually, I do have a note from Ms. Quinn, but he doesn't really give me a chance, so I say, "If that's what makes you happy," and he sends me down to Ms. Quinn for being rude.

"So where were we?" I ask her, getting comfortable on the sofa.

Chapter 24

ANGELINA'S WEDDING DAY comes fast, and the stress that I feel over the cleavage dress is further emphasized by the fact that even the priest looks down at my chest when he's giving me instructions.

But I take a deep breath and I do the comparison thing. People are dying of hunger and terrorists are creating fear, and evil politicians are taking advantage of that fear and refugee kids are drowning trying to come to our country and Mia can't even go to her favorite niece's wedding, and the list goes on forever.

Suddenly a cleavage is *nothing* but me being pathetic. So Pachelbel's Canon starts and it's my cue.

The ushers open the door and I step inside.

And I step right back outside again!

Will Trombal is in the fifth-last row, third person from the end. I can't breathe.

"Frankie?"

The whole bridal party is looking at me.

"I can't go out there," I tell them.

Angelina lets go of my uncle Rocco's arm and steps forward. The others are stunned.

"Brides and grooms are allowed to have second thoughts. Not bridesmaids," Vera explains in her duh-brain voice.

Angelina holds up her hands as if to say, *I'm trying to stay calm.*

"I'm in a pretty bad mood, Frankie. My mother-in-law's from Queensland and she wants to toast the Queen at the reception and Angus doesn't want to upset her, but he's fine about upsetting me. I want desperately to have a cigarette and I've promised Angus that I'll give up smoking on our wedding day if he gives up his Old Boys rugby shorts. At this exact moment, I feel like that cigarette. *Don't let me begin my marriage as a liar.*"

The others are looking at me pleadingly. One does not upset Angelina on any given day, let alone her wedding day. After a moment I nod. I've seen Angus in the shorts. They should have been thrown out fifteen years ago when he graduated from high school.

So I walk in.

Don't look at him. Don't look at him. Don't look at him.

I look at him. We don't make eye contact, because he's looking at the cleavage.

After the ceremony, my nonna tries to pin my dress to cover me up, relishing the absence of my mother. Of course Will sees all this, and I begin to wonder when my humiliation will be complete.

At the reception hall, things get bad. Toasting royalty is a completely foreign concept for my extended family. Although they can relate to the fact that Queen Elizabeth doesn't get on with her daughters-in-law, they're just not interested in paying homage to her and they chat through the whole thing. Worse still, Vera the gym junkie is flirting outrageously with my father and he's laughing with her. She's attractive and uncomplicated, and she does the helpless thing well. Mia's never been helpless until now.

From my lonely spot at the main table, while the bride and groom are socializing and the maid of honor is breaking up my parents' marriage, I watch as Will introduces his family to Luca, and I can almost hear them saying how adorable he is. Luca sits down and he's the center of their world and I feel invisible and ugly and, more than anything, I miss Mia. I miss sitting with the grown-ups, the way she included me in their conversations. If it wasn't her, it was usually Angelina, but she is too busy being a bride tonight.

My partner remembers that I'm alive and asks me to dance to "Nutbush City Limits," and Tara Finke invades my body and I tell him that standing up and dancing the same steps as everyone else in the room, en masse, is the last bastion of conformity.

I don't see him for the rest of the night.

I go into the toilet and sit on a chair, staring into space. In one of the cubicles a line of smoke comes over the top, and I look underneath the door and see the ivory dress.

"Angelina?"

The cubicle door opens and she ushers me in. Thank God she didn't do the big poufy dress and there's room in there for me as well.

Next to the toilet there's a window, and we poke our heads outside. She hands me the cigarette and I take a drag.

"I'll be gone two months," she tells me. "So you've got to take care of Mia."

I nod.

"Listen to me. It's not your fault. It's not Uncle Robert's. It's not Luca's. And most of all, it's not Mia's. Sometimes your whole system just shuts down and you wake up in the morning and everything's black and no matter how much people speak to you and try to talk you out of it and tell you everything's okay, it doesn't work. Mia is going to get out of this thing, Frankie, but it's not going to happen on the day she gets out of bed or the next day or the next. And there are some days you're going to find it hard, but you have to be there for her. Get her back into a routine and she'll do the rest somehow. And whatever you do, don't underestimate your father. He's been married to the clueiest woman I know for eighteen years. That means he has to be cluey himself. Your parents' marriage works because of your father as well, Francesca, not just because of Mia, and she'll get out of this because of Robert and you guys. Just don't give up on her."

She takes out some breath freshener and sprays it in her mouth.

"You're beginning your marriage with a lie," I tell her.

"I went through his overnight bag in the limo. He's packed the shorts."

"Enough said."

She washes her hands and wipes them and gives me a kiss, and then she's gone.

I fix up my makeup and step outside. Will is standing there, as if he's been waiting.

"Nice dress."

I roll my eyes.

"No, really. The . . . the color . . . it . . . it . . . it looks great on you."

"They're called boobs, Ed," I say, quoting Julia Roberts in *Erin Brockovich*.

He grins, and after a moment he takes both my hands in his. "Are you okay?"

I shake my head. Lying to Will takes up too much strength. I just want to blend into him.

He bends forward and kisses me and I let him. I love the rough feel of his suit against my bare arms and the smell of him and the bristle of his chin.

He presses me against the wall and I feel every part of him imprint itself on me, but after a moment I feel myself pushing him away.

"I can't do this if you have a girlfriend, Will. I just can't."

He's silent for a moment, but it's like he can't find the words. "It's complicated."

"How?"

"Whatever I say is going to make me sound like a bastard. It's just not that easy."

I pull my hand away. "Nor am I."

But we're still touching, our foreheads together.

"I'm supposed to be going overseas next year. Just to add to the complication," he says.

"For how long?"

"A while. But I don't know. . . . I kind of like my comfort zones, you know. I don't really think I want to leave that behind."

I wonder if he means "leave her behind."

"Comfort zones are overrated," I tell him. "They make you lazy."

He smiles. "You come out with weird things."

The MC announces the speeches and we walk back into the hall, where he introduces me to his parents. They're a bit older than my parents, and very friendly.

His father looks inquiringly at Will. "Sophia?" he asks.

Who the hell's Sophia? Even my mother, who doesn't know what day it is, knows Will's name because I talk about him all day long. His family have no idea who I am.

I excuse myself politely and walk toward my father, and we dance. Luca attaches himself to my waist, and the three of us sway as the Elvis impersonator sings "It's Now or Never." I remember when I was younger and my mum and dad would be holding Luca in their arms and I'd attach myself to them and we'd dance all night.

But tonight one of us is missing and, combined, we feel like an amputee.

Chapter 25

I CAN'T GET the Will Trombal kiss out of my mind. No. "Kiss" is not the word to describe it. The Will Trombal experience. The Will Trombal extravaganza.

"Up against a wall?" Siobhan whispers during class.

"Shhh. And I said there was a wall there, I didn't put it in those words. You make it sound like a sex thing."

"As if it's not."

"Shhh."

"Can you stop shushing me?" she says, irritated.

Mr. Brolin is speaking totems and serpent rainbows like he has no idea.

"Don't let him use you," she whispers.

I look at her, not believing I'm getting this piece of advice from someone whose experiences are well documented on the wall of the boys' toilets. She is offended by the look.

"I do *not* let them use me," she says forcefully.

"You go out with so many guys and it never works out and

then you end up crying in a bedroom at a party."

"So what? I need to be on the lookout for 'the One.'" She does the quotation-marks thing with her fingers.

"Well, my 'One,'" I say, wiggling my fingers back, "has a girl-friend."

"You don't know 'the One's' girlfriend, so there's nothing un-ethical happening," the Queen of Ethics explains.

Our fingers are beginning to hurt.

"That's not true. Because teenage girls who steal boyfriends today will be stealing husbands in ten years' time. I'm a home wrecker in training."

"Oh please. The guy can't keep his hands off you and you blame yourself."

"If I had a boyfriend," I tell her, "and I felt for Will what I think we both feel, I'd split up with my boyfriend. And he's not doing that."

"If he does, he might be losing a friend," she explains. "The girl could have been a friend first."

"So he and I don't happen instead?"

She shrugs. "I went out with this guy once. Remember Nick Fox on my street? Best friends for years. We had the same taste in every-thing, and I just loved talking to him and making sense of everything with him. But I realized I just wasn't interested in him romantically, so after an agonizing six months I broke it off with him, and he never spoke to me again. Very sad. Second time in my life that my best friend stopped talking to me."

She gives me one of those meaningful looks.

"You're the one who came back in Year Seven with the 'you are so naïve' attitude," I argue.

"Yeah, but that didn't mean you had to let the Body Snatchers invade you," she snaps.

"Can you not call my friends the Body Snatchers?"

"Let's not make them the point of this conversation," she says with a sigh. "Let's just focus on Will."

Mr. Brolin stands in front of us.

"Twenty minutes, this afternoon," he says coldly.

"Why?" asks Siobhan.

"Detention," he says, putting it into quotation marks with his fingers.

As usual, Jimmy Hailler is on detention, as well as Thomas for listening to his Discman in class.

"Caught smoking today," Jimmy tells us. "With Will Trombal."

"*What?*" I *so* don't believe him.

"That boy's bad," Jimmy continues. "B-b-b-bad to the bone."

"Will Trombal and you were sharing a cigarette? Doubt it very much."

"Go ahead, Thomas. Live up to your name."

"Then why isn't he here?" I ask.

"Why would he be?"

Jimmy speaking to Will is a dangerous thing. It makes me almost break out into a sweat.

"What were you discussing?" I ask.

"Weddings."

I'm beginning to feel uneasy. I look at Siobhan, stricken.

Brolin pops his head in to see if we're working, and then he's gone.

"I love weddings," Jimmy explains. "I don't go to enough, and we were looking at it from a cultural standpoint and of course the music. Trombal feels that there aren't enough Elvis impersonators in the world."

"Did he mention Francesca?" Siobhan asks.

"No. The world doesn't revolve around Francesca being felt up by Will Trombal against a wall outside a toilet."

I look at Siobhan again, this time horrified.

"Who's got the big mouth, Siobhan?"

"Oh, like I'd tell this little shit anything."

"Why would Will want to talk to you?" I snap.

"I offered him my cigarette and said, 'Let's talk women, Will. How does one sustain two at the same time?'"

I'm seething and Brolin's back. The moment he disappears I lean forward and whack Jimmy across the head.

"He's making all this up," Thomas says.

Jimmy shrugs, rubbing his head. "People tell me stuff, what can I say. Didn't you once tell me that you get turned on whenever a certain someone—"

Thomas almost jumps over me to get to Jimmy before he says another word. Suddenly Siobhan and I are intrigued.

"You people need to take a chill pill," Jimmy says. "That's what I told Trombal as well. He told me something important, which I can't for the life of me remember, but I remember what I said. I said, 'Trombal, you need to loosen up, man.' And then we got busted by Mr. Portell."

"Busted smoking?"

"So we spoke cars. Trombal's brothers are car hoons and have a Subaru WRX, which seemed to impress Portell, so by the time the mention of detention came along, Portell did the warning finger,

171

confiscated the cigarettes, and is probably smoking them as we speak."

"So what are you doing here?"

"Hanging out with you guys."

I'm shaking my head. "You are not coming home with me, Jimmy."

"Don't be so cruel, woman."

We stand packed on the bus with Tara and Justine, who waited for us. Justine is squashed, further down the bus, between two very large people, and she constantly waves to remind us that she's there.

"You are not coming home with me, Jimmy," I tell him for the fourth time.

"Trombal's coming to camp," Thomas tells me. "It'll give him a chance to cheat on his girlfriend again."

"Camp," Jimmy explains, totally ignoring me for the fourth time, "is one of two things I hate most in the world. The other is role-plays. Sometimes it's a double whammy. You go to camp and you have to do a role-play. 'Role-play a scene with conflict, gentlemen,'" he says, adopting a teacher's voice. "And then you have to sit through ten role-plays where a kid comes home drunk and his parents confront him at the front door."

"I like the idea," Thomas says. "I've never been to camp with chicks before."

"Must you always refer to us as animals? If we're not chicks, we're birds or dogs," Tara complains.

"Or cows," Thomas adds.

Tara rings the bell with an exaggerated middle finger and prepares to get off the bus.

Siobhan looks at Tara. "If you were in her shoes and Will Trombal had kissed you twice and not committed, what would you do?" she asks.

"I'm not into relationship advice," Tara explains.

"Based on the fact that she's never had one," Thomas scoffs.

"Neither have you, except for the one with your hand."

I'm impressed. So is Siobhan.

"That was a great call, Tara," Siobhan says.

Tara is pleased with herself and gets off the bus.

People start moving down the bus and we're packed in more than ever.

"Oh my God," I say, pushing Thomas out of the way. "It's the tuba guy."

"The what?"

"This guy that Justine likes. He's in the same youth orchestra as her, but she's never spoken to him. He looks at her at the bus stop every morning, but there's no way that he'll ever know her name because she's so tongue-tied around him."

"Those relationships go nowhere," Thomas says. "Six years down the track you're still referring to her as the 'chick with the ponytail at the bus stop.' Tell her to stay away from it. It'll only end in heartbreak."

The tuba guy reaches us. Up close, he's probably less attractive than from a distance, but there's a lovely honesty to his face.

"Justine?" Thomas calls out to where she has just managed to escape being wedged against the door. She looks over at us, smiling, and the moment the smile disappears and is replaced by a stricken stunned-mullet look, I know she's seen Tuba Guy.

"There's room over here," he says, pushing Tuba Guy. "Oh, sorry, mate." The apology is so earnest that I actually believe for a moment that he did it accidentally.

"No worries," Tuba Guy says, making room.

Justine reaches us, her face flaming red.

"You looked squashed over there, *Justine*," Thomas says.

She doesn't answer him. Thomas isn't trustworthy material. He is uncomfortably nose to nose with Tuba Guy.

"Is that a Sydney Boys uniform?" he asks.

Tuba Guy nods slowly, trying to act cool.

"Do you know Chris Hudson in Year Eleven?"

"He's in my biology class."

"Tell him Thomas Mackee said to say hi. And *Justine* and Francesca," he says, pointing to us.

"And Jimmy," Jimmy says, shaking his hand. "What exactly is a tuba made out of . . . sorry, what did you say your name was?"

"Francois."

"Francois? French, I presume. Have you ever watched *Queen Margot*? There's this fantastic St. Bartholomew Day's massacre scene."

Justine is pinching me on the hip and I try hard not to flinch.

"Jimmy?" I warn.

Then it's their stop and Tuba Guy says the magical words.

"After you, Justine."

Jimmy puts a hand to his heart and feigns an "isn't this romantic" look. Thomas is making kissing sounds, and I can't believe I'm stuck with them both.

"You're not coming home with me, Jimmy."

At home, Jimmy has a polite thing happening with my mother. She sits in the sunroom and he's talking tea and fantasy fiction with her.

"I gave up caffeine when it started making me jittery," he explains to her. "I'm a bit of an expert, Mia. My nan used to swear by chamomile and it helped her heaps."

Jimmy never asks questions about Mia. Why she's in her nightgown every time he comes over. Why she looks so thin and tired. He isn't even curious. Just matter-of-fact and comfortable. Sometimes he has this yearning look on his face when he's speaking to her, like a little boy.

"What can you recommend for the fantasy booklist?" she asks. She's determined to hold on to the conferences, but the reading is hard work. Lately, I've taken to typing her notes out for her. She has a laptop from the university, and whatever she says I type. Then I take it to school and Tara reads it over, giving me suggestions. Siobhan, funnily enough, is the grammar queen and works on the style.

Luca sits on the arm of her chair and shows her his art portfolio.

"Eddings, obviously, and Irvine. Heard of him?" Jimmy asks. "And of course the *Obernewtyn* stuff."

Mia looks up from the portfolio as I put some toast in front of her.

"Are you a fantasy reader, Rob?" Jimmy asks my dad, who's been standing at the door, watching.

"I don't have much time to read, *Jim*."

I can see my mum's mouth twitching and it gives me a bit of hope. My father always seems a bit tense when Jimmy is around. I don't know whether it's because Jimmy's a guy or because Jimmy gets more of a reaction out of my mum than anyone else, but his coldness makes me feel on edge.

"I'd read fantasy if they had simple names like Jane and Bob from Wagga," I say. "Why does it have to be Tehrana and Bihaad from the World of Sceehina?"

Jimmy looks at my mother and rolls his eyes. "No wonder they call her a bimbo behind her back."

And my mum laughs.

And because of that, Mark Viduka, the soccer player, stops being my brother's hero, and Luca and Pinocchio run after Jimmy like he's their idol.

"Don't you ever wonder why she's always in her nightgown?" I ask Jimmy as I'm walking him up to the bus stop. He looks at me. Not like Will looks at me or the way Thomas perves. He just looks, and I don't know why, but I get tears in my eyes.

"It just means she's not going anywhere. What's wrong with that?" he says with a shrug.

"Did your mum go somewhere?" I ask.

"Mine? She's . . . just a loser, you know."

I've never known someone with a loser mum.

"Does she live with you?" I ask.

"I'm with my grandpop these days."

"Do you miss—"

"No."

He shrugs again, as if he doesn't give a shit.

I just stare at him. I want to ask him a thousand questions, but I can tell he doesn't want to be asked.

"We make weird friends," I say instead.

"I've never been into the f-word with people."

"I'm privileged, then? Why me?"

He thinks for a moment and then shrugs again.

"You're the realest person I've ever known."

"Is that good or bad?"

"It's fucking awful. There's not much room for bullshit, and you know how I thrive on it."

We laugh for a moment and begin walking again.

"You girls are weird in a way. I would never have spoken to Trombal or Mackee or even Shaheen, whatever his name is. They would never have spoken to me. Everyone used to be so different to each other, but with you girls here, everyone kind of just hangs out."

"Maybe it's just Year Eleven or being somewhere new. I was the same with Justine and the girls."

We sit at the bus stop for a while, just talking.

"I don't miss her," he says, thinking about my earlier question about his mum. "But I miss . . . I don't know. Being held, you know?"

He rolls his eyes, but there's a blush thing happening on his face.

"Do you want to hear something that will cheer you up?" he asks.

I shrug.

"Are you ready?"

I nod.

"I played Captain von Trapp in Year Four."

"You did not."

"Yeah, I did."

The bus comes toward us, and as we stand up he breaks out into "Edelweiss" and he sings it loudly and dramatically, his voice wavering with mock emotion.

And I hug him, holding him tight. At first I think I'm doing it for him, but then I don't want to let go, so he does the letting go.

He gets on, singing to the bus driver, and the doors shut and I can see him walking down the aisle serenading various people, who look on, bemused. He sits in the back row and opens the window.

"By the way, I just remembered what Trombal told me that was so important."

The bus pulls away and I'm jogging beside it.

"He split up with his girlfriend," he yells out.

He breaks out into song again and I stand there, hearing it all the way up the road. And then I bolt, straight home, my heart singing. Will Trombal has no longer got a girlfriend. I dance around the kids skating on their grind pole and race straight up to the house and I call Justine. Because we have men in our lives and there's much to talk about.

Chapter 26

MEMORY IS A funny thing. It tricks you into believing that you've forgotten important moments, and then when you're racking your brain for a bit of information that might make sense of something else, it taps you on the head and says, "Remember when you told me to put that memory in the green rubbish bin? Well, I didn't, I put it in the black recycling tub, and it's coming your way again."

Today I'm in the music room, waiting for Justine, watching her play a piece for her music teacher. The tune isn't important, although I recognize it as one of the classical pieces from an advertisement, but it's watching her that fascinates me. Her fingers are on keys and buttons, at the same time knowing exactly when to squeeze the accordion in and out, and for a moment I think she's making it up, that all she's doing is putting her fingers anywhere and yanking it back and forth, but then all of a sudden it works and it blows my mind. Her eyes are closed and there's a look of absolute bliss on her face. When have I ever felt that peace?

It was the first week of Year Ten. Restless with my friends gossiping about the guys on the 8:00 a.m. 438 bus, I was walking past the drama room, where they were having tryouts for the Year Ten musical, *Les Miserables*. I stood at the door and watched as five musicians played an overture, and I remember Justine Kalinsky, her eyes closed, that look of bliss on her face, those fingers flying over the accordion keys.

When Mia came to pick me up from school that afternoon, there was something different in the air. It was two months after her father had died, and I remember how beautiful she looked that day. Not that I wasn't used to her looking beautiful, but Nonno dying hit us hard for a while and I hadn't seen her smile for ages.

It was like some fantastic aura was surrounding both of us. "So give me a rundown," she said as I fastened my seat belt.

That's what she always said, and I usually shrugged because I had nothing new to tell her. But that day I turned in my seat to face her as she drove through the suburbs, and I took a breath.

"I'm going to tell you something, but I don't want you to get excited," I said.

"I can't promise lack of excitement, Frankie. You know that."

"Okay, the school's going to do *Les Miserables* and I've decided to go for the part of Eponine."

She nodded approvingly. "Interesting."

I was crushed. I stared at her, hardly believing her reaction.

"Aren't you excited?" I asked her. "You've been nagging me for years to get involved in a musical."

We stopped at the lights and she looked at me, laughing. "You told me not to get excited!"

"As if I mean it! You've ruined my moment."

"I'm not excited, I'm ecstatic," she said, pinching my cheek.

"It's not as if I don't know all the songs by heart," I explained, getting the information out of my bag.

"Eponine is a big role."

"You don't think I can do it?"

"I'm petrified that you can and I'm going to be in the audience blubbering."

I grinned, determined and so sure of myself.

"You know how Nonno used to sing those folk songs at all the parties? Well, it's like he invaded my body. Do you know what I mean? Maybe this is his way of saying goodbye," I said.

She looked at me for a moment, and there were tears in her eyes, and she nodded and then laughed.

"I know exactly what you mean."

I looked at her knowingly. "So what's your news?"

"What makes you think I have news?"

"I don't know. You seem different. You have a glow."

"What would you think if I told you that I'm not going to take the UTS job just yet?"

"How come?"

"I think I want to stay home for a while."

I was a bit shocked. "Really! Since when?"

"Since I don't see enough of you guys, and when I do I'm marking or tutoring."

"As long as you don't drive Daddy and us crazy."

She laughed. I don't know why, but I joined in, and we sang songs from *Les Mis,* dramatically, at the top of our voices, all the way home.

The next day at school I told Michaela and the girls about the musical.

They did this thing where they looked at each other and their eyes did a bit of a roll.

"What?" I asked.

"The musical?"

"Yeah?"

"It'll take up your afternoons," they said. "What about our plans to play basketball at the Police Boys' Club with the Burwood boys?"

"Maybe we can do that next term."

"That's a bit selfish, Francis. Postponing something we've planned with them just because of one person."

"We desperately need you," Laura said. "You're our tallest player."

"I'll work around it," I promised.

"Anyway, girls in the choir are going to go for the musical. They've got fantastic voices."

"Mine's not that bad, you know."

I could see them looking over my head again, but I don't know what look they were exchanging.

Three weeks later, I stood in line with my audition piece. If you're going to audition for Eponine, you do "On My Own," and luckily Luca and I have inherited good voices from my mum's side of the family. I had hammered every note at home, and I felt confident. But I was also uneasy, and the idea of my friends coming to school with all the stories of playing against the boys, and all the fun I'd miss out on, made me feel sick. As I watched the competition, the pit inside my stomach grew bigger. I was better than these girls and I was going to get that part. I was more sure of that than anything else.

So I walked out.

At the door, I came face to face with Justine Kalinsky, holding her accordion.

"Where are you going?" she asked.

"I've changed my mind."

She clutched my hand. "You can't."

But I walked past her and stuffed my audition piece in my locker and met my friends and listened to them have a discussion about how gorgeous Natalia's hair was, and that afternoon when I got into the car, it was as if Mia knew, because the mood was so different from three weeks before. I lied to her and told her that I didn't get the part, but I don't think she was listening.

"I'm going to take the university job," she told me flatly.

"You don't seem happy."

"I'm just tired. A bit sad, you know."

She was fighting back tears but tried to smile.

"I'm a bit sad too," I told her.

And we cried all the way home. Just sobbing together, almost hysterically, and I pretended that I was crying because of my grandfather and because I didn't get the role of Eponine, and she told me that she was crying because she was so torn about staying home and hanging out with us in the afternoons.

Both of us were pretending.

And I know why I was, but I can't work out what her reason was.

Chapter 27

MY DAD FORGETS to pick up Luca and me from a nighttime recital at the cathedral, so we make our own way home. At 10:30, I hear the key in the door and wait for him to come in.

"Where have you been?"

He looks surprised to see me standing there.

"I went to a council meeting. Why aren't you in bed?"

"Since when have you gone to council meetings and since when have they finished at 10:30?"

"Since Mia couldn't. And I was giving Hildy and Emma some advice about their wall foundations." He's still in his work clothes, and I'm following him around as he pulls off his dirty boots and puts them outside.

"Oh great," I say, "now the whole neighborhood is going to talk about what you're getting up to with other women."

He walks back into the house and looks at me, stunned.

"They're lesbians, Frankie. There's nothing to talk about."

"So if they weren't lesbians, there'd be something to talk about?"

"Why are we having this ridiculous discussion?"

He opens the fridge and takes out some stuff for a sandwich.

"How do you know they're lesbians, anyway? Are you an expert now, or do you just go around generalizing like every other ignorant person out there?"

"Oh, so now I'm ignorant? When did this come about?" he snaps.

"When you started laboring under misapprehensions about two women with short hair who choose to live together," I say, trying to use as many big words as possible.

"You mean the two women who said to me, 'Would you be able to draw up some building plans for the Gay and Lesbian Association that we belong to?'"

He looks at me as if to say, are you finished now that I've won this discussion? But I won't let him win.

"You forgot to pick us up from the recital."

"Shit," he mutters to himself. "Did Luca get home okay?"

"Thanks to me he did. He thinks you're not interested in his choir stuff."

He disappears into Luca's room and he's in there for a while.

I'm trying to calm down, but I can't. I don't know why I'm so upset. Mia forgot to pick us up tons of times, and I never questioned her when she came home from a council meeting.

He walks out again and continues making his sandwich. Once upon a time, I would have done that for him.

"Why did Mummy take the job at the university?" I ask him.

"Because it was offered to her."

"But for a while there, she wasn't going to take it. At the beginning of last year. She was going to stay home. Why didn't she?"

"I don't remember, Frankie. Go to bed. You're tired."

"Whenever you suggest things, it's always about putting away the problem but not fixing it."

He turns and looks at me.

"I'm not going to have this discussion with you while you're upset," he says evenly, but I can tell that deep down he's seething.

"We're never going to have this discussion, are we?"

"Go to bed."

"I can't believe you're going to pretend that everything's okay!"

"I'm not going to say it again."

"Luca and I are sick of pretending. We're sick of no one telling us anything. What's going on in his head is probably worse than the truth, but you don't care."

"I don't care? About you and Luca?"

"You just care about us when everything's okay, but when it's not, you don't even know who we are!"

I'm hysterical now, but I can't help it and I don't want to stop.

"Keep your voice down!"

"Or what? The neighbors will find out that you can't fix everything?"

"What do you want from me?"

He shouts it and we're both stunned. For a moment I feel as if it's not me he's shouting at.

Is it Mia? I can't tell.

And I hate him and love him and curse him and feel sorry for him, all at the same time.

Chapter 28

THE THEORIES ABOUT why Will hasn't asked me out are getting wilder by the end of the week, but Siobhan's suggestion is the most ridiculous.

"It's not another woman," she says.

I'm already shaking my head. "He's not gay, Siobhan."

"It's God."

We're sitting on the bus and I hear Thomas groan behind us.

"Why couldn't I have lived in the eastern suburbs?" he says.

"How is it that you can listen to that crap and us at the same time?" I turn to face him for a moment, and he puts the Discman on full blast.

"Please explain," I say, turning back to Siobhan.

"It's simple. Remember the video we watched about people joining the nunnery?"

"Convent."

"Whatever. Remember one of them said she went around, her mind tortured for months while she was making the decision. She had to tell the guy she was dating as well as her parents, who desperately wanted grandchildren." Siobhan looks at me. "He's going to join the priesthood or the brotherhood."

"That's the most ridiculous thing I've ever heard," I say.

"Why?" she asks.

"I can't imagine Will Trombal a bridegroom of Christ," Thomas says, poking his head between the two of us.

"Why? He goes to a Catholic school. He's been there since Year Five and he used to sing in the choir, so he's spent a lot of time in church. He's never embarrassed about doing anything religious, like reading at our paraliturgies, plus he's split up with his girlfriend and still hasn't tried to make a move on the other woman in his life," Siobhan says matter-of-factly.

I look at Tara, because despite her rantings, she's the voice of reason.

"Do you think it's true?" I ask.

"No. But if it's not, what's his problem? I don't think he knows what he wants."

"Way to go, O sensitive one," Thomas says to her.

Justine is looking at me with that empathetic face of hers.

"She's got a point. When I realized you liked him, I watched him, just to see what you saw in him, while we were at church for the Feast of Edmund Rice, and I noticed that after he was given communion he did the sign of the cross."

"A lot of people do."

"But he did it," she says, looking at all of us, nodding her head, "as if he *meant* it."

The idea that God works in mysterious ways is rubbish. There's nothing mysterious about his ways. They're premeditated and slightly conniving, and they place you in an impossible situation. How can I pray to God not to let Will Trombal join the priesthood? God's not going to do me any favors here. I'm in a lose-lose situation.

Thomas puts his arms around my neck. "You've still got me."

"Don't upset her any more than she already is," Siobhan says.

I throw myself into drama. I've decided that when I grow up, I want to be an actor. There's something so powerful about being elevated on that stage and looking out and not having to make any eye contact, and despite what Tara says, as female roles go, I don't think it gets better than Lady Macbeth. Unfortunately, I'm not even close to being the star. The guys who play Macbeth and Macduff are fantastic and act me off the stage. But I reckon that Lady Macbeth gets the best lines, and I make the most of them.

"Find your range," Ortley always says to me. "Don't play her mad from the beginning because you'll have nowhere to go."

"Are we going to do a musical next year?" I ask him.

He looks insulted. "This is drama. The music department takes care of the musicals."

"Isn't it all the same thing?"

"Go away," he orders. "Rehearse the part where Lady Macbeth throws herself off the balcony."

Thomas is cast as Banquo and is not impressed.

"He's dead by the second act," he argues. "I'm better than this."

"He comes back as a ghost, though," Ortley says placatingly.

"And he calls his son Fleance. Anyone who calls his son Fleance deserves to die."

"Tom, I want you as Banquo," Ortley says, sitting him down.

"Does he get a fight scene?"

"He certainly does."

Thomas is still not convinced, and he's less impressed with me than anyone else.

"Why do you get to say, 'The raven himself is hoarse that croaks the fatal entrance of Duncan,' and I get to say, 'Fly, Fleance, fly'?" he asks, sulking.

I can't believe he knows my lines by heart. "If you want to play Lady Macbeth, it's yours," I tell him as we walk out. At the end of the corridor I see Will speaking to Brother Edmund outside his office.

"Probably asking if he can borrow his wardrobe," Thomas snickers.

I look at him, unamused.

Brother Edmund walks into his office just as we reach Will, so Thomas does the sign of the cross in exaggerated reverence and Will gives him the finger.

Somehow I doubt very much that Will is joining the brotherhood.

Chapter 29

IT'S SCHOOL CAMP time. A sense of helplessness comes over me as my dad drops me off at school. I look at Luca in the rearview mirror and wonder how he'll cope over the next few days. What about my dad? Who will he speak to or argue with? Who will make Mia's chamomile tea just the way she likes it? I feel nauseous, and it's not just because I'm thinking of the reflection sessions and trust games. I know I'll spend my whole time there thinking of home, worrying about the family not coping with me gone. What about Mia? Just say she goes backward while I'm at camp. Not that she's moving forward rapidly, but sometimes, lately, she's been on the phone speaking to a friend or even listening to Luca read.

My dad is whistling cheerfully, putting on an act, I'm sure, and Luca is out of the car and running toward his friends playing marbles before I've even opened the door.

"I'll call every day," I tell my dad.

"Don't be ridiculous. You'll only be gone three days."

He gives me a peck on the cheek. "Quickly, before this bus drives over us."

Will and a band of merry prefects are in charge of this nightmare. They're the only Year Twelves attending, and I think they've been given a pep talk on keeping enthusiasm high.

"If they get any more cheerful, you'll see an upchuck on the Princes Highway," Jimmy Hailler mutters.

Ms. Quinn comes along and taps him on the shoulder.

"Let's check through your bags to see if you've packed neatly, James."

He gently pushes on her shoulder, effeminately.

"Let's."

If Jimmy's stashed away anything, I doubt they'll find it.

Brother Louis, wearing jeans, stands alongside me.

"Love the denim," I tell him. He looks pleased.

We get the lecture about no alcohol, no drugs, no cigarettes. "Zero tolerance," they say. They warn us that they'll send us home in a taxi and let our parents pay for the two-hour fare. Anyone found in a cabin with a member of the opposite sex will be suspended. They've been listening to the all-famous "What to threaten students with at school camps" tape, which must be circulated to all schools.

When we arrive at Gerringong, down the South Coast, we're told to get into a group of eight and grab a cabin. The four of us stay huddled together. The girls standing closest to us we call the Hair Bear Bunch because of their fascination with their hair—it's all they ever talk about. The Indie girls are on the other side of them. They're the type of girls who would consider me a social outcast if they knew of the presence of a Britney Spears album in the Spinelli household. Rumor has it that Tara almost joined their group but they found out she had the Celine Dion single "My Heart Will Go On." Tara reckons they protest for the sake of protest, and we agree that we couldn't bear listening to Socially Aware FM for the next three days. Thankfully, Eva Rodriguez's group grab us in our hour of need, and we bag cabin number one.

Camp is so outdated, it's retro, and I doubt it's changed much in thirty years. I can guarantee we'll end up singing "Peace Train," "Imagine," and "Let It Be" before the night's out. But I enjoy it because I need something to stop me from thinking about home.

Thomas and his friends have brought along their guitars, and they play their punk crap in the food hall. I can't believe I know all the lyrics, thanks to sitting next to him on the bus every day.

Tara, Justine, and I stand watching them, their only audience.

"Someone should tell him that he can't sing," I say.

"Oh please. Let me," Tara snickers.

"I can play that," Justine muses.

"On the piano accordion?"

"What are you laughing at?" she asks me.

"You blow me away."

Having boys around at camp is hard. You have to be on the alert. Boys, for example, like exposing themselves. They walk back from the shower blocks with their towels around them, and next minute either someone flashes at you, or one of his friends grabs his towel off him and makes a run for it. I have to say it's a bit traumatic at times, not knowing when the next penis will appear.

The first night I have to help Ms. Quinn and Brother Louis serve dinner, and they are as relaxed as, laughing with each other and the helpers. I try to work out what I like about them. There *are* cooler teachers and even more stimulating ones, but I think it's the fact that they actually like us.

"Are you married?" I ask Ms. Quinn.

"No. You?"

I laugh.

"If I can't have Brother Louis," she tells me, "I don't want nobody, baby."

I look at Brother Louis, who has two pink stains on his cheeks. It makes him look so cute.

"I'm in love with someone I can't have as well," I tell them boldly.

"He's a fool," Brother Louis says to me.

I'm pleased.

I get a bit of a crush.

It's lights out at ten o'clock, which is when the action starts. The other girls in our cabin have a CD player, and someone puts on some music and Eva Rodriguez shows us how her brother hip-hops. "It's like world peace is determined by how serious you are and how low you wear your pants," she tells us.

It starts off ridiculous and goes downhill from there as we each take a turn. We dance in a way that's only possible when there are no boys around. The rule is not to take yourself seriously, but whoever gets a solo has to keep as straight a face as possible and go for it.

Siobhan, Eva, and I try to outdo each other and everyone's laughing uncontrollably, even Tara. We collapse on our beds, perspiring.

"God, you're a show-off," Siobhan tells me between pants, still laughing.

"Takes one to know one," I say back.

Later, we lie on our bunks, talking in the dark. About anything. We go around the room, nominating teachers we love; teachers we hate; Year Eleven boys we'd date; Year Eleven boys we hate. Guys or girls we suspect are gay. We have a massive debate about which *Buffy* season was the best and an Angel versus Riley versus Spike dispute, and we end up nominating our most romantic moments in a film.

"*The Last of the Mohicans,*" I say. "Daniel Day-Lewis, Madeleine Stowe. 'Stay alive. I will find you.'"

"Drew Barrymore in *Never Been Kissed,*" Justine says, "waiting for the guy out on the baseball field and she doesn't think he'll show and that Beach Boys song comes on and he's running down the stairs and everyone's cheering."

". . . and Justine's crying," Siobhan says.

"Every single time. I've got it on DVD."

"Han Solo and Princess Leia pretending to hate each other in *The Empire Strikes Back.*"

"Boring," one of the girls boos.

"Don't *ever* insult the *Star Wars* films," Tara warns mockingly.

"In *The Godfather* Michael Corleone sees this girl in Sicily who ends up being blown up by the Mafia, and the look on his face is priceless," Siobhan tells us.

"When she's getting blown up or when he first sees her?"

"Buttercup and the Farm Boy in *The Princess Bride,*" Anna Nguyen suggests. "'As you wish.'"

"Jason Biggs and the apple pie."

We groan.

"No, I've got the best," Eva Rodriguez says. "*Jerry Maguire*. 'You had me at hello. You had me at hello.'"

That one gets applause, and it trails off until the last two voices are dreamy blurs.

I think I'm a bit in love with these girls. They make me feel giddy. Like I haven't a care in the world. Like I'm fearless.

Like I used to be.

Don't get me wrong. The camp does hit a few low points. We have to make a human pyramid displaying the foundations of the Catholic Church, and the most frightening aspect, according to Brother Louis, is that Thomas Mackee is holding up the pyramid, which makes the whole future of the church incredibly shaky.

But I get to know people I have never spoken to. Some tell me that they thought I was weird until now, or that it's the first time they've seen me smile, and for a moment I feel like the most popular girl around. And then they ask me if I could introduce them to Siobhan or Eva.

After dinner on the second night, we hang out in our cabins listening to music until we hear a scream from outside.

"Probably another penis sighting," I tell Justine as we walk out to investigate.

Will and the prefects are standing in front of a cabin, two doors down. The girls from that cabin are crying hysterically, and the prefects look harassed.

Obviously a hair-grooming session has taken place, as the girls are all braids and beads. Ryan Burke comes up behind Tara and me and puts an arm around our shoulders.

"What is it with girls and séances?" he asks. "My sister has them all the time."

Justine is trying to calm the girls down.

"We were trying to contact Eliza's grandfather, but now there's an evil presence in there," one of them cries.

"Who? The Blair Hair Witch?" Tara mutters.

Ryan and I look at each other comically.

"Did she just crack a joke?" he asks.

The Hair Bear girls refuse to go back into their cabin.

"There are *no* other cabins left," Will explains politely, but the girls aren't budging and I can tell he's pretty shitty.

"Spirits are easy to get rid of," I inform them. "You go in there, say eight Hail Marys while walking counterclockwise."

Will and the prefects are not impressed. It's obvious they got little sleep last night, and their eyes are hanging out of their heads. The séance girls, however, are looking at me as if I'm their hero.

I walk up the stairs to the cabin and Will follows me, but I gently push him back. "Nonbelievers are barred." I look out at the crowd. "Believers, come forth!"

Tara, Siobhan, and I exit the cabin. We've spent ten minutes inside, hip-hopping while chanting a few prayers with mouths full of the Twisties and Pringles we found lying around.

We stand on the veranda and everyone below us stares in silence. Justine is still comforting one of the Hair Bear girls, and Eva and the rest of our cabin are killing themselves laughing.

"This house," I say dramatically, like in a scene out of *Poltergeist,* "is clean."

We get a massive cheer and applause. We wave a royal wave, and the Hair Bear girls are grateful and instantly our best friends, promising us free makeovers.

Will is looking at me, shaking his head with bemusement, as the others go back to their cabins.

"What?" I ask.

"You're psychotic."

"I got them back into the cabin, didn't I?"

"What have you guys been doing in there? You're perspiring."

"Hip-hopping."

He looks at me, as if he's trying to work out if I'm having him on.

"You don't strike me as a hip-hopper," he says, laughing.

"I squeeze it in between ghost-busting."

I look down at what he's holding in his hand.

"Fart gas? Shame on you, Will."

"Tom Mackee's cabin. There could be more."

"As if they don't have enough natural emissions of their own."

I feel reluctant to go and he seems to feel the same. It's pitch-dark and we can only see each other's outlines. We sit on the veranda and his hand comes across and touches mine and I slip my fingers through his and we sit like that for a while.

"What are you thinking?" he asks.

I'm thinking heaps of things, but they all require too much honesty and I don't think I can take that at the moment.

"I'm wondering who came up with the concept of putting fart smells in a can."

"Worse," he says, hardly able to stop himself from laughing, and I just love the sound of it. "Imagine being their kid. Imagine going around saying, 'My dad invented fart gas in cans. That's how we made our millions.'"

It degenerates from there and we try to outdo each other's gross-ness until he yawns and apologizes, and I can sense his tiredness.

"How much sleep did you get?"

"Hailler, the dickhead, got chucked out of his cabin because he wouldn't shut up, so he ended up in ours and continued to not shut up for the rest of the night."

"What did you guys talk about?"

"Rugby."

"What else?"

I can sense his surprise. "Nothing else, just rugby. You?"

"Lots of stuff. And then movies. Have you ever seen *The Last of the Mohicans*?"

"I love it."

"Really?" I'm over the moon. We share a movie. Finally, we're on the same planet.

"Don't you love the part where he says, 'Stay alive. I will find you'?" I ask.

"I love that massacre scene," he says, like an excited little boy, "where they're walking down that path in the middle of nowhere and they're surrounded by the woods and you know the Indians are going to attack and it's so tense."

Things that make you go *hmmm*.

I can sense him looking at me in the dark and I turn to face him, feeling the warmth of his breath on my face.

"What's going on, Will? Speak to me."

I don't know where those words have come from. I've heard Mia say them. "What's going on inside your head, Rob? Tell me."

Will doesn't speak, but his hand squeezes mine tighter.

"It's like you have a plan and someone comes along and makes you want to change it all, but you still like your first plan, no matter how fantastic the second one makes you feel."

"I've never planned anything, so I don't understand the feeling," I say.

"Well, I plan everything. I even plan my plans."

"So tell me about plan number one."

"First of all, but not in this order, there's civil engineering. I know I can get between approximately 98.6 and 99.3 in the High School Certificate and that analyzing King Lear's nervous breakdown on the heath is going to be the deciding factor in those marks."

I can sense him looking at me in the dark as if I'm supposed to understand this dilemma.

I'm in love with a droid! Any minute now he's going to start using formulae to work out how he feels about me.

"I know I want to kind of run away next year. Do the whole backpacking thing. Just get lost, you know?"

"You were so confused about the whole overseas thing and now you're so certain," I say. "Aren't you worried about leaving your comfort zones anymore?"

"It's like what you said at the wedding. About comfort not being everything."

Great. Now he's going to start taking my advice, when it'll mean him leaving.

"I need to sort out the plan priority," he says decisively.

"Tell me about plan number two."

"I stay and hang out with this smart-ass who can tell me the difference between Trotsky and Tolstoy."

I want to beg, "Pick plan two. Pick plan two."

He kisses me and it's not like at the party or the wedding. It's soft and slow and familiar, and this time around I feel as if he's in control of how he's feeling and that there's no regret or guilt on his part. But I taste a bit of sadness in that kiss and I don't know whether it's mine or his, but it makes us both tremble and not want to let go.

I sit next to Jimmy on the way home, and he teaches me how to play Nintendo with the precision of a surgeon.

"It's hard, but you'll get the hang of it," he says, handing it over.

I beat him first go and I hand it back. He looks at me darkly.

"You've frightened me in the last two days, Francesca. I want you to go back to your pathetic self as soon as possible," he says.

"Why?" I grin.

"Because you being pathetic makes me feel good about myself," he jokes.

In front of me, Thomas and Justine are sharing a Discman, one earphone in each of their ears.

I put my face between them.

"Tuba Guy's not going to be happy," I say, doing the smooching sounds that Thomas always does when I'm speaking to Will. Behind me, Tara and Siobhan are asleep, heads against each other, mouths hanging open, a bit of saliva on the side.

I feel a wave of sadness come over me. I want the bus driver to turn the bus around and I want to spend the rest of my days in a whirlwind of the last few days. Of flirting. Of laughing. Of ridding the world of evil. Of folk songs. Of piggybacks. Of hip-hop dancing. Of foolishness.

And most of all, of forgetting.

I look past them to where Will and his friends are sitting, and he catches my eye for a moment and smiles. It's a weird smile, but it reaches his eyes and I bottle it. And I put it in my ammo pack that's kept right next to my soul. The one that holds Mia's scent and Justine's spirit and Siobhan's hope and Tara's passions. Because if I'm going to wake up one morning and not be able to get out of bed, I'm going to need everything I've got to fight this bastard of a disease that could be sleeping inside of me.

Chapter 30

I TURN SEVENTEEN. It's on a really bad day for Mia. One of those days that make me think she'll never get better. Some days aren't just a step back, they are a mile. This morning she's crying and it's painful to hear and my ears ache from the sound of her sobbing. I can hear my father's voice, comforting her, like it always does. But the heart-wrenching sound doesn't stop. There's just so much grief there, and I stick my pillow over my head and wish the day away.

No one remembers it's my birthday, and I'm glad because I just couldn't bear putting on a smile and pretending to be happy about being a year older. The Stella girls don't ring. No one rings. Not my grandparents, not anyone, and the worst thing is that it's Sunday and I'm not at school with my friends, and it's the loneliest day of my life.

Birthdays in the past were spectacular. If it wasn't a thousand presents, it was a dinner out, and the birthday person got to choose. Mia let us have wine and we'd make toasts. People would look at us and I could hear them say, "What a great family!" Were we too smug? Does God punish the smug? Does what we had automatically transfer to some other family who didn't have it but now do, courtesy of our despair?

My father walks into the kitchen. "Go take Luca up to the Abouds." No "please," no softness toward me in his voice.

"And then where do you want me to hide?" I ask snidely.

He stares at me, but I don't care because I don't know who he is anymore. I used to see him smile every day, but I haven't seen him smile for months. People used to always say he should grow up, but a grown-up Robert isn't fun. *Bring on the immaturity,* I want to say. He's still staring, and for a moment I don't recognize the look in his eyes.

"You blame me for this, don't you?" he says.

"Luca!" I call out, still looking at my father, straight in the eye. "The Abouds want you to come over."

"Don't you?" he persists.

"I don't need to. You're doing a better job."

I walk up the road with Luca and Pinocchio.

You blame me for this, don't you?

I can't get the words out of my head, both his and mine. Deep down, when I analyze how I feel, I realize that there is resentment and it's not toward Mia. It's toward my father. It's like this bubble that's inside me that I keep thinking is going to burst on its own because it's too weak to withstand. But it's not. It just builds up and builds up, and every word that comes out of his mouth, every feel-good sentiment, every bit of optimism, makes me want to yell hysterically. And in this whole mess, this whole period of everything aching, it's thinking this way about him that makes me feel as if I'm slowly bleeding inside.

* * *

201

On Monday, the only thing that gets me out of bed is the fact that I hate this house so much that I'd rather die than stay here.

I spend the day on Ms. Quinn's sofa. Once upon a time she'd work quietly, put off phone calls while I was in there and not allow anyone to disturb us. Now she's become so used to it that life goes on around me. The normalcy of routine in that office, in itself, is a comfort.

At one stage I have no idea what time it is. I wake up and Will's sitting on the floor, his back in front of me, leaning against my sofa.

"Hey," he says quietly, leaning back so our faces are level.

I can hardly speak but I try. "I was born seventeen years ago," I tell him. "Do you think people have noticed that I'm around?"

"I notice when you're not. Does that count?"

I close my eyes again and go to sleep.

When the afternoon bell rings, Justine is standing outside Ms. Quinn's office, holding my bag. I bet she's carried it around all day.

Our group of four walk across the park in silence. At one stage, Siobhan bumps me with her hip. It's one of those are-you-okay bumps. I bump her back. Already I'm feeling a bit better, even though I dread the idea of going home. As we walk through Grace Bros., Justine drags me to one of the cosmetic counters.

"Let's get makeovers," she suggests.

"Waste of money," Tara says. "All we'll be doing tonight is homework."

"Francesca?"

I nod. "Why not."

When it's over, the four of us rave about how beautiful we look. Even Tara is fascinated with herself.

"I've got the best idea for tonight," Siobhan says. "Thomas is going to watch some band down at Coogee. He said we could come along. It'll be fun."

"It's a school night," Justine argues, getting that pink stressed tinge in her cheeks.

"We're celebrating." Siobhan grabs my face. "It was her birthday. Look how sad she looks."

I think for a moment. "What band?"

"Some punk band he's into."

I look at Tara and Justine hopefully.

"We won't get in," Tara says firmly.

"We will," Siobhan says. "I'll get us in."

"The lying's too complicated," Tara argues.

"Only because you make it complicated," Siobhan complains.

I can tell that Justine is having a stress attack at the idea of it.

"It'll be fun," I say, trying to convince her. "I can tell my dad I'm staying at your place, and you can tell yours that you're staying at Tara's, and so on and so forth," I plead. "You can ask Tuba Guy as well. This is your opportunity to ask him out, Justine. It's a music thing. It'll make sense."

"And how do we sneak back into my house without my parents hearing?" Tara asks.

"I'm the expert," Siobhan says, clapping gleefully. "Leave it to me."

Thomas and his friends and Jimmy meet us outside the hotel at 7:30. Tuba Guy has arrived before us and is already being terrorized by Jimmy, who I can tell has just asked him his hundredth question.

"You look great," Tuba Guy says as we stand around. But he's mostly looking at Justine.

"It's just the makeup," Tara says in her practical tone, because I can tell she's embarrassed by the attention she's getting from the guys.

"We know that, Tara," Thomas says. "We've seen how ugly you look underneath it all." But he is staring at her. Sometimes, I think he has a crush on all of us but it is Tara who makes his heart beat fast, although he'd rather die than admit it.

We walk inside. The place is semi-packed and we try hard to look discreet. The band is set to play in another room at 9:30, so we decide to make ourselves comfortable in the lounge. Jimmy shouts out to someone he knows, and we push him into a booth.

"We're trying to be inconspicuous," Justine says.

"Chill," Thomas says as we make ourselves comfortable. "You chicks get hot and bothered about anything."

"Why is it that you always sound like someone out of a bad seventies movie?" Tara asks him.

"Because I'm trying to compete with the I-Am-Woman-Hear-Me-Roar image you have, Helen."

"It's Ms. Reddy to you."

We discuss who is going to get the drinks.

"Tara and I will go," Siobhan says, having already eyed the young bartender.

Thomas puts two fingers together and does a smooching sound.

"Maturity, Thomas," I warn.

There's something so exciting about doing something illegal. You feel as if the whole world is looking at you, but no one really gives a damn. When a waitress comes to clear the table next to us, Justine starts babbling about the university degree she's doing.

"Huh?" Thomas asks. "What is she talking about?" he asks me.

I kick him under the table and Jimmy's killing himself laughing, very loudly.

When Siobhan and Tara come back with our bourbons, we make a toast.

"To Francesca!"

They raise them up in the air as the waitress comes back.

"On her nineteenth birthday," Justine blurts out.

"Did she repeat?" Tuba Guy asks, confused.

"So did Trombal give you anything?" Jimmy asks, nosy as usual.

"A compliment. That was enough," I say, thinking of him in Ms. Quinn's office.

"Trombal doesn't know how to give compliments," Thomas says. "The other day I'm trying to put some work in for you, Francesca, and I'm saying that you look like the chick in the toothpaste commercial, you know, the one with the short dress and the big tits?"

I'm ever so slightly horrified.

"Please don't assist me in any way, Thomas," I beg of him.

"Well, Trombal's like, 'No. She looks like Sophia Lauren' or something like that, and I'm thinking, you loser! Here I am trying to pay her a compliment and you can't even pretend that Francesca's hot."

"Did he just insult me?" I ask Justine.

"Yes, but the tragedy is that he thinks he's paying you a compliment."

Then something clicks into place. "Sophia Loren?" I say, remembering Will's father calling me Sophia at the wedding.

"You've heard of her?"

"Sophia Loren is, like, the most beautiful woman in the world," Tara tells him. "She's an Italian actress."

"Then why haven't I heard of her?"

"Because you're too busy watching toothpaste commercials. She's, like, in her sixties. . . ."

"He's comparing you with an old person? He has no idea."

"How can we explain this to you, Thomas?"

"He's not going to get it," Siobhan says, already bored.

"Let me try." Jimmy faces Thomas. "From what I can remember from this film, *The Boy and the Dolphin,* Sophia has big tits."

"Ahhh," Thomas says, nodding.

"Is that all you guys notice?" Tara asks, disgusted.

"No. I'm actually a great ass man myself," Jimmy explains, just to rile her up. "What about you?" he says, turning to Tuba Guy, with that evil/innocent look on his face.

Tuba Guy looks stricken, and Justine looks like she wants to dig a hole.

"The piano accordion thing does it for me," he mumbles quietly.

Tara, Siobhan, and I look at him proudly. Justine's face is just about pink.

The band comes and the music is mindless, but I feel on track with everyone in the room. The whole space is a mosh pit and I sway, courtesy of five hundred other people around me and the alcohol. The world from this perspective is strange, and for a moment I stand in the middle of it and just absorb it. I can smell the dope and the body odors and the beer and the spirits and the puke. I can smell Justine's perfume as she puts her arms around me and we move to the beat and everything is a strange blur of bodies. I think I imagine it, but this one time when I open my eyes I see Tara and Thomas and I'm sure something's happening between them, some kind of touch, some kind of look, but it's gone so quickly and the mirror ball spins and my hair is matted to my forehead. And the way I feel about everyone in my life is so clear. It's almost like an epiphany.

Later, we pull Siobhan away from the bartender at the pub, who's just walked off his shift.

"What??" she says, looking at us innocently.

"Can we not go anywhere without you picking up someone?" Tara asks, hailing a cab. We all crawl in.

"Am I hurting anyone?"

"Yourself."

"How?"

"You're the one who gets upset, Siobhan," Justine says.

"Only with the name-calling. Not with anything else. That time at the party, it was the name-calling that made me cry."

I lean against Justine.

"Did he kiss you?" I ask.

"No. I kissed him."

We grin at each other.

The taxi driver pulls into Tara's street.

"Oh God," Tara says, quickly yanking off her seat belt. "There's a police car outside my house." She's almost in tears. "Oh God. Something's happened to my parents."

Siobhan grabs her arm. "It's my father," she says flatly. "We're in for it."

The taxi stops and none of us move.

"You have no idea how much trouble I'm going to be in," Justine says.

"What's the worst-case scenario?" Tara asks.

"Try no weekends for about a month, which means I don't get to go to Canberra with the orchestra."

"Canberra's not that exciting," Tara says.

"Tuba Guy," I explain.

She nods, understanding, and we get out of the cab.

"I'll tell them it's my fault," I say. "I'll tell them the truth. That this morning I felt like crap, like I could have just walked in front of a bus. . . ."

"Don't say that!" Justine says, and under the streetlight, I see tears in her eyes. "Don't ever think that, Francesca."

"Promise," Tara orders me.

"Cross your heart," Siobhan pushes.

I put my hand on my heart. "I swear on the Holy Bible."

They still look tense, and I smile.

"Chill. You chicks get hot and bothered about anything."

I get dropped off home in a police car. Siobhan's father lectures us all the way about drinking. The epiphany is wearing off and is replaced by a blinder of a headache. I walk into the house and my father is sitting in the kitchen, in the dark. I don't switch on the light because I don't want to see the look on his face.

"You got a card in the mail," he says. "It's in your room."

I don't say anything.

"For your birthday."

That's all he says and I figure it out. Realizing that they missed my birthday, he would have rung me at Justine's, and that's how they would have worked out our ploy.

He doesn't shout, he doesn't say anything. It's as if we've got nothing left to say to each other. So I go to bed and I feel so sad that I have to psych myself out of crying. *Think happy thoughts,* I tell myself. *Think happy thoughts.*

I think of Sophia Loren.

Chapter 31

THE STELLA GIRLS are on the bus the next morning, and they do the same thing they always do when they see me. They're theatrical and affectionate and excited for approximately fifty seconds, and then their attention is diverted. I don't feel like being cheerful or upbeat with them because Justine is so down about her parents' punishment and I feel guilty.

"Where have you been?" they ask. "We haven't seen you for ages."

I shrug.

"What did you do to your hair?"

That means they don't like it. People who ask that question make it obvious how they feel. Funny how they liked my hair when it stayed the same for four years and the moment I change it they hate it.

"Remember in Year Seven when it was cut really short and everyone called you Frank?"

No. I remember Year Seven when my mother would grab my face between her two hands and say, "I love this little face that I now can see." Or how Nonno Salvo would ask, "Where did those eyes come from?" I remember being called beautiful for the first time.

Why do they always have to remember the pathetic stuff? Why can't they ever remember something positive being said about me? I remember Jimmy saying that me being pathetic makes him feel good about himself. From him it's a joke, but for the Stella girls, it's true.

"Did we ever play basketball with the Burwood boys?" I ask them.

They look confused.

"Remember? In Year Ten we were going to play at the Police Boys' Club after school."

"Why do you ask?"

It's not that I think they're mean. I just don't think they notice when I'm not around.

"Oh my God," Michaela says, clutching my hand. "Your birthday!"

I shrug.

"What did you do?"

"Nothing," I say.

I don't want to share it with them. I realize at this very moment that if I never see these girls again, I wouldn't care.

I glance at Justine and she looks hurt, and I'm confused until it hits me that she misinterpreted my answer. It's our stop and she gets off the bus without a word.

"Wait," I call out to her, but she's already gone.

The Stella girls are looking at me, surprised.

"Do you hang out with Justine Kalinsky?"

I nod. "Worse. She has to hang out with me. *Poor thing.*"

* * *

I decide to go and see Will before school starts. I've had it with this waiting business. I can cope with another woman, but I can't cope with being ignored when there's nothing in his way.

I knock at the prefects' office door and one of the others answers.

"Will, it's for you," the guy says, smirking. I stare him out and he stops smirking and excuses himself.

"Are you okay?" Will asks, standing up.

I nod.

We stand facing each other and that stupid, looking-at-Will heart-thumping starts. *Get over it,* I want to tell myself. He's just a gawky guy with a cowlick, not some stud.

"Don't even think about it, Will."

"Think about what?"

"Think about what you're thinking about."

"Why do you have to do that?" he explodes. "Why do you have to take a perfectly logical mind, with a touch of so-called intelligence, and turn it into mush?"

"You're about to kiss me, Will. I can tell because I've been kissed by you enough times to see the signs. Your face goes all pinched, as if you're in battle, and you almost grit your teeth. What am I? A nightmare for you?"

He resigns himself to the fact that I'm not going away too soon and sits down.

"You're like these trays," he says. "In-tray, out-tray. Unexplainable. You're unexplainable."

"You're comparing me to stationery?"

"I'm comparing you to . . . rugby and . . . my voice breaking . . . and everything I love but don't understand."

"To the failures in your life."

"No. I'm comparing you to all the things I love doing best and I just can't have when I want them."

I pull up a chair and sit down in front of him, our knees touching. I take his hands, squeezing them.

"Ask me out, Will. Because if you don't, I'll have to ask you out, and I have a feeling that you're going to analyze why you can't go out with me and it'll make you feel like crap to say no."

He leans forward to kiss me, but I shake my head.

"It'll be easy," I tell him. "Next year I'll be here, you'll be at college. . . ."

"I'm not going to be here next year," he says, sounding frustrated. "I told you that at camp."

"But you had to sort out the plan priority."

As usual, I get the full impact of his stare, and it's all there in his eyes. The whole truth.

"So the plan without me won?"

He shakes his head. "It's not about you . . . actually it is about you, but for all the right reasons," he says.

"You go out with some girl and you're so torn about going overseas, but the moment I'm interested, it becomes so clear to you that going overseas is a fantastic idea. Thank you very much, Will. Welcome to the people who have made my week such a great one."

"It'll only be a year."

"How can it be so easy for you to decide?" I cry.

"I can't believe you think that!" he shouts.

"What am I supposed to think? You spend all your time trying to stick your tongue down my throat, and the moment I want something more, you decide you need to go away."

"This isn't about you. It's not personal," he says.

A cold fury grips me, but my heart's already sunk before I can save it.

"Everything to do with me is personal," I say, hardly able to get the words out.

I walk out.

I need voices of reason and of hysteria and of empathy. I need to have an Alanis moment. I need advice from Elizabeth Bennett. I need Tim Tams and comfort food.

I need to find the girls.

Tara's the only one in homeroom when I arrive, and I'm kind of relieved. She always looks at things to do with other people's lives objectively.

"You did nothing for your birthday, did you?" she snaps, furious.

At first I'm confused. Too much has happened since this morning on the bus. I realize that Justine's told her about my conversation with the Stella girls.

"I didn't want to talk to them—"

"Why does someone who gives so little think she deserves so much?" There's a pinched anger in her face. It's not that bitchy look I remember from the Stella girls when they were picking fights. It's pure anger, and it's all directed toward me. I see Siobhan making a beeline for us from the other side of the room, and I'm relieved that there is going to be some kind of reprieve.

"You're a bitch, Francesca," Siobhan says when she reaches me. "Why don't you just go to Pius, where your 'real' friends are?"

I sit down at my desk and slowly take out my books. Justine walks in and sits where she usually does, next to me. I look at her, but she won't look at me. I can tell she's miserable.

"Justine, I didn't—"

"I don't want to talk about it, Francesca."

I nod, and I feel tears welling up in my eyes and my lip trembling. I haven't been friends with them long enough to be able to withstand a test. You pass tests like this five years into a friendship. But I think, this is it. This is going to be like in Year Seven. One day they're going to say, "Remember how we were friends with Francesca Spinelli for two terms in Year Eleven?"

Or worse still, one of them will answer, "No. Who's Francesca Spinelli?"

I can hear them talking about Justine's punishment from her parents because of last night. Her parents won't speak to her, on top of everything else. For Justine, that's the worst thing.

The bell rings.

I'm numb. I walk the corridors in a daze and then there's the exit sign and I just walk out. I go past the secretaries, past the front gate, past everything. Through Hyde Park, through the city, down Market Street, over the Anzac Bridge, and up Johnston Street.

I sit in a café in Booth Street and just stare into space until, after a while, I feel someone standing next to me and I look up and recognize Sue, Mia's colleague from work.

"Thought it was you," she says. I force a smile and she sits down.

"How's Mum?" she asks gently. I just shrug, not really interested in lying.

"She gets out of bed sometimes," I mumble.

"You know what I think?" she asks.

Just what I need. A theory from one of Mia's friends.

I shrug again.

"The last eighteen months have been tough for her, Francesca, and with your grandfather dying and starting at the university at the same time as the miscarriage . . . Mia needs a vacation."

She keeps talking but I no longer hear what she is saying. My head is reeling from just one word. Miscarriage.

My mother had a miscarriage? Mia lost a baby. We lost a baby. I can't work out a word Sue is saying. It's garbled and in another language. A language spoken by those who just don't understand.

I stand up blindly and do what I've become an expert at today. I walk away.

I'm dead inside and I feel as if the world's ending and I need to get home and I walk faster and faster because the people across the road will wave to me and only then will I know everything is fine but when I get there, they're not there like they are every afternoon and every morning and every night and I want to know why because they have to be—because if things aren't normal with them, things aren't normal with me and I want to run over and bang at the door and tell them to come outside and eat their dinner on their laps or lean over the fence and speak to their neighbors and I want things to be exactly the same as they always were because if they are, the world is still turning and at the moment I feel as if it's stopped turning and I can't stand feeling this way and I go inside and my father is standing there.

"What are you doing home, Frankie?"

I don't know who he is anymore. I don't know who anyone is.

"Why didn't you tell us about the miscarriage?" I ask.

I see him stiffen for a moment and he doesn't answer.

"Hello?"

"Don't *hello* me, Frankie. We didn't want to upset you."

"Well, I'm more upset by the fact that you kept it from me."

"It was over a year and a half ago."

"I know exactly when it was. It was what I was trying to ask you about the other day, but you lied."

"There was too much going on and we didn't want to—"

"Did you ever talk about it with her?" I interrupt.

"She didn't want to talk about it."

"She always says that. 'I don't want to talk about it.' She's said that a thousand times."

"And I respect that."

"But it means that she *does* want to talk about it!"

"I know Mia. I know more—"

"No you don't," I snap.

"What are you trying to say?"

"She's not part of you. She's part of us."

"Don't you dare say that."

"You know nothing!"

"I'm not going to have a fight with you."

"I bet she wanted to talk about it."

"I don't want to talk about it."

His shouting makes me jump, but I don't back down.

"Yeah, but maybe she did. And maybe she wanted to talk about

Nonno dying, too. And maybe you didn't let her. You do that all the time. You blow everything off."

I'm hysterical. I don't know what I'm talking about. But I can't stop.

"You keep her all to yourself. You think you can fix everything by forgetting about it, but you just make things worse. It's all your fault. You've kept her sick, because you don't know how to handle it. Because you're a weakling. Everyone says you are, and I believe it and Mummy could have done better than you and I don't know why you just don't *fuck* off now before you make it any worse."

The look on his face is so devastating, but I don't care. I want to hurt him.

I turn to walk out but my mum is at the door, looking horrified.

"Don't you *ever* speak to your father like that *again.*"

I run out of there, to the people across the road, and I bang at their door over and over again, but no one answers and I keep on banging until there's blood on my knuckles and then I run up the road as fast as I can because I need to find them.

But I don't.

They're gone.

I hear my father calling out my name, but I keep on running.

Everyone's gone.

And I need to find them.

Chapter 32

I DON'T CARE where I end up. I walk to Central Station and get on a train and then I sit there, watching the stops pass me by, all their names meshing into one, until the stops become infrequent and I know I'm out of the metropolitan area and I have no idea where I'm going or when I'll get there. It's like one of those mystery flights, except I'm in no mood for surprises.

I have two dollars on me and, in all probability, a fare evasion fine awaiting me on the other side of wherever. After what seems like hours, the train stops, but I don't move. There's not one other person in my car and I feel like the last person on earth. Finally, I step out of the car and look at the sign. Woy Woy. We've driven past the sign before on the way up to the coast with my mum and dad and Luca. The Woy Woy sign in the past was a good memory and I want to remember it, but I can't and I say the words over and over in my head, hundreds of times, sitting there for hours and hours, trying to remember why the Woy Woy sign in the past was a good memory. But I'm not remembering anything at all. I'm just saying words in my head that mean nothing.

People appear again. It happens all of a sudden. One minute there's nobody and next minute a train pulls up and hundreds of people get off and I realize that it's rush hour and, like most of my days, I wonder where time has gone. I look at some of their faces closely, but they don't look at me. They just walk or rush or talk or laugh, their heels tapping toward me, then in front of me, and then they pass me by. And that happens at least every half hour. The same thing. Not one person looks at me. They want to get home. It's written all over their faces. And I keep on telling myself that after the next train comes I need to move. Need to do something, because it's dark and my skin feels cold. But my brain has stopped ticking and I can't even think of how to do that. In reality, it's all about turning around and getting on the train on the platform behind me, but the first casualty of all this is the ability to operate logically.

And then a train comes and nobody gets off. Not one single soul, because everyone's home. I don't know whether they're happy there, or angry with the people they live with, or waiting for something good to happen, but they're someplace better than here. I want to go home. I go back to saying *Woy Woy* over and over in my head until I realize that it's Mia's name that I'm saying, and my dad's and Luca's and Will's and Justine's and Siobhan's and Tara's and Jimmy's and Thomas's and Ms. Quinn's and Brother Louis's and Mr. Ortley's, and then I start all over again. Their names ringing through my head.

And in that dark silence where it seems that everyone is someplace but me, it all comes back. Mia and me on the beach when I'm twelve. She's telling me a story of when I was five and I almost drowned. She calls me Frankie the Brave.

"I don't remember," I tell her as we watch my dad and Luca out in the surf on the boogie board.

"You had this gorgeous pink bikini with flowers attached at the side and shoulders, and you were throwing yourself across the surf like the insane kid that you were and then running back to us and saying, 'Did you see that, did you see that?'

"All of a sudden, we heard a scream and we realized that someone was out there drowning. Robert raced down the beach and I knew he'd be okay and that he'd get whoever was out there. But then you bolted down after him. You pulled those flowers off your suit and threw them to the side, and you ran straight into the water because you had to save your father. You went under and I couldn't see you and I was screaming and screaming, but you didn't come up again and I thought, my baby's dead. . . ."

I remember. Being Frankie the Brave and then years later being Francis the Fearful. But more than anything, I remember my dad's hands. Out there in that surf. I knew they were his, even with all that water pounding in my ears and down my throat and even though every wave was like a giant punch against me, I knew his hands. And then I was holding on to his shoulders, my arms tight around his neck, my legs wrapped around his waist, and the fear just vanished.

I stand up, sure of one thing and one thing only. That my father will come and get me. He won't give me a lecture, he won't try to teach me a lesson. He won't ask a thousand questions or ask me to apologize. He'll just come and get me. I find a telephone and put in the two-dollar coin and the phone only rings once and I say, "Hello."

"Just tell me where you are."

I don't know how it happens, but not even a minute later the police pick me up from the phone booth. They take me back to the station and make me a cup of Milo, and they are so kind.

"Your father will be here soon."

When I grow up, I think I'm going to be a cop. They're nicer when you see them up close, and I love the idea of driving around neighborhoods picking up teenagers who have sworn at their fathers and evaded train fares.

It's well after midnight when my dad walks into the police station and I start to cry. Just seeing his face makes me cry. He hugs me and doesn't say a word, and then I'm in the car and he's driving me home.

On the way, we stop at one of those rest stops for gas and food, and we sit at a table opposite each other. I can't speak. I'm scared to. I'm scared that anything I say will make him look the way he did yesterday, and I'm scared he'll leave because of me.

"I didn't want the baby."

I don't know what to say, so I say nothing. I let him speak because I have a feeling that it's the first time he's said it out loud.

"But Mia was ecstatic and she'd say, 'This is a sign, Robert. My father's died and we've been sent this baby.' Then she had the miscarriage and I felt so guilty, as if I had willed it to death."

I shake my head. Is this what he's carried around all this time? This guilt and sorrow?

"When she wanted to talk about it, for me it was a reminder, so I'd brush it off."

His voice sounds choked and I can't bear it.

" 'Everything's going to be fine,' I'd tell her. 'If you want, we'll try again.' Because I'm sure that's what someone who's been pregnant for twelve weeks wants to hear. That the baby she had lost could be easily replaced."

I touch his hand and he grabs mine and squeezes it, not letting it go.

"I don't know what to do," he says. "I don't know how to make this right."

And it's that very moment, looking at him up close, that I realize the truth.

"I've been scared all this time that we'd lose her," I say to him. "That maybe we'd come home one day and she would have killed herself or something. But then I guessed she wouldn't, but I just felt scared inside all the time. And then I realized that it wasn't just losing Mummy that was scaring me. It was losing you, too. I thought, just say he gets sick of it all? Just say he leaves? I always thought Mummy kept things together, but you did, Papa. You always did and I just don't know whether we'd cope without you."

"I'm not going anywhere, Frankie. What's happened to Mia"—his voice cracks and there are tears in his eyes and I can't stop crying—"it kills me. But I would never give up on Mia or you or Luca. Just don't give up on me."

"Fathers in the movies always say they won't leave and then next minute they're packing their bags and moving in with uncomplicated women who spend a lot of time at the gym."

"I'm not a father in a movie."

"It's because you're our optimist," I explain to him. "And most of the time that's fantastic, but sometimes you don't let us talk about how we're feeling. If we feel scared, you say, 'Nothing to worry about, guys,' but that doesn't make it go away. It makes it grow. And that's what I was trying to say yesterday. That maybe she wanted to talk to you about the baby and about Nonno and about not coping and you kept saying, 'It's going to be okay, Mia.' And maybe she didn't want to be told it was going to be okay. Maybe she just wanted to talk to you about it."

"That sounds too simple."

"No, it's not. I think not being able to talk to you is probably the scariest thing in the world for her. If *I* couldn't talk to you, I'd want to die."

He's crying and although I can't bear it, I try hard not to cry.

"I think it's about her grieving and you have to let her talk and you have to talk to her back."

"When did you get so smart?"

"Oh yeah, I'm so smart. That's why I'm God knows where and my friends who I thought were my friends aren't, and the ones who are my friends, who I never considered my friends, aren't talking to me, and the guy I'm in love with isn't happy enough putting a girl between us but now has to put a body of water between us."

He looks a bit stunned, but he smiles. "When you were born, I was hoping that the dramatic streak would skip a generation."

"I'm not being dramatic. It's the truth."

"Your friends are at the house."

I sit up straight. "Who?"

227

"I don't know. Weird people. The Sullivan girl, whose father got the Gosford police to pick you up."

"Siobhan?"

"And another one who's making cups of tea for everyone and keeping the boy who's telling Luca fart jokes away from the girl who says he's 'the last bastion of patriarchal poor taste.'"

"Justine, Thomas, and Tara."

"And the drug fiend, Jimmy, is keeping Mia calm, and the Trombal boy's called about ten times. I don't like his manner on the phone."

"You won't like any guy's manner on the phone."

He slides out of the booth and takes my hand, pulling me against him as we walk out.

"Tomorrow, let's try to get Mummy out of the house," he suggests.

I nod. Saturday morning at Cafe Bones doesn't sound too bad.

"Do you think I look like Sophia Loren?" I ask him as we get into the car.

"I used to tell your mother she looked like Sophia Loren." He looks at me, frowning, and then it registers. "Oh God, some guy's using that line on you, isn't he?"

"Not just 'some guy,'" I tell him. "*The* guy."

We get home and Mia and Luca hold me so tight that I feel as if I can't breathe, but in a way I've never felt so alive. My friends are still there and my dad lets them all stay the night, even Jimmy and Thomas. None of us get any sleep because everyone's got a different account of the last fourteen hours, and they make it sound like a movie of the week.

"Brolin's like, 'Where's Francesca Spinelli? I saw her in roll call this morning. She's cutting, isn't she?' And he marches down to Quinn's office and she throws a Quinn-fit and tells him to get a life—"

"That's not true," Siobhan interrupts. "She says, 'Doug'—I'd change my name if it was Doug—she says, 'Doug, Francesca's going through some issues at home. Let's just try to find her. . . .'"

"Trombal told Shaheen, who told Eva that Quinn told Bro that Brolin was a 'detriment to the students.'"

The five of them have an argument regarding the truth.

"That's not true," Tara says. "Shaheen and Eva aren't even speaking to each other at the moment."

"What's up?" Thomas asks.

I can't get over how easily these guys get off track.

"*Hello,*" I yell over their voices as they discuss the Shaheen/Eva dispute. "It's not about Brolin or Quinn or my mum or my dad anymore." They stare at me. "It's about me and the fact that I've felt like crap for so long and not just this year. That's the weird part. This year has been one of the best years I've ever had and I might win the uncoolest-person-of-the-year award by saying this, but if you weren't my friends, I think I'd just go into some kind of coma."

Justine has her arm around me and I'm crying my head off while I'm telling them, and then I see Thomas roll his eyes.

"God, you're uncool," he says, "for even thinking that. Now can we stop talking about such trivia and talk about the real issues?" He makes himself comfortable on my bed and looks around with this stupid demented smile on his face. "So who's sleeping with me?"

* * *

229

I lie in my mum's bed, facing her, and I remember what Angelina said. That she's not going to get better just because she gets out of bed.

"Are you and Daddy going to be okay?" I ask her.

"Why do you ask?"

"Because people grow out of people. You've known him for over twenty years."

"I've known you for seventeen and I haven't grown out of you and I never will. Why should it be different for Daddy?"

"Because I'm your flesh and blood."

"Oh God, Frankie, I breathe in rhythm with that man. You think that's not my flesh and blood after all these years?"

We hold on to each other and she looks at me closely, as if she hasn't seen me for a really long time.

"When I was seventeen," she says, "I just stopped speaking to my father for two years. I thought he was a peasant, some kind of idiot. I was embarrassed by how simple he was. I was such a bitch. But all I can remember now is his face—his beautiful patient face, waiting for his daughter to start speaking to him again. He never questioned what was going on and he never pushed, and I saw that as a weakness. But he was just waiting."

Her thought process is written all over her face. It creases her forehead and makes her mouth look hard and twisted. I try to press it out with my fingers. If I just smooth out those creases, she'll go back to normal.

"I grew out of it and that was because of your father. Seeing the world through Robert's eyes is incredibly soothing, though I have to keep on pulling myself away, because I need to use my own eyes. But thanks to Robert, I saw Nonno for what he was—this beautifully simple man who knew exactly what he wanted in life—and I envied him for that. . . . 'Clarity,' I think, is the word. But I never told him that. I thought that one day I'd sit him down and tell him how sorry I was . . . and I never did find the time. And if I could just have *one* minute, just to say goodbye to him, I would never complain again, Frankie. *Never.* And I thought when I got pregnant last year . . ."

One day I'll ask my mum about that baby. If she already had loved it or what she imagined our lives would be with it around. And what's missing in our lives without it. But for now I let her talk. I try to wipe her tears away, but there are too many.

"I just want to wake up in the morning and for the light to be on," she sobs, "and I want to stop feeling like a success just because I can eat my toast and I want to be able to brush my teeth without throwing up and then when I get through all of that, I want to work at getting that look out of your eyes. That look of fear that I put there and I hate myself for that."

"But when we're happy, you put that look in our eyes as well. So you have to give yourself thousands of brownie points for that," I tell her.

She lets me trace the scar on her stomach. The scar I put there when I was born.

"It's because you were in such a hurry and I wanted to have you all to myself for just a little while longer," she murmurs sleepily. "Even back then we were battling each other."

When I grow up, I'm going to be my mother.

chapter 33

THE NEXT MORNING, I see Thomas, Jimmy, and Siobhan off in Tara's father's car. Justine is meeting Tuba Guy and opts for the bus.

"Tara's driving is a nightmare, anyway," she whispers in my ear.

We stand on the pavement, listening to Thomas and Tara squabble.

"How about we don't turn all this into a tragedy and you let me drive, Tara?"

"How about no."

"You mean yes/no or no/no?"

"You just want to drive in my father's Commodore."

"No. I just want to live until my next birthday. Is that too much to ask?"

"Is it too much to ask that you guys don't argue the whole way home?" Jimmy says.

Justine is laughing and I'm loving the sound of their voices.

Siobhan sticks her head out of the window.

"I love youse."

Thomas leans over and beeps the horn, and I see Tara slap his hands away.

They drive off and Justine kisses my cheek.

"I'll ring you later. Maybe if my dad lets me, we can meet down at Bar Italia for a gelato tonight."

"Cool."

I watch her walk up the road, and then she disappears and my anxiety returns, just for a split second. And somehow I find myself running, and by the time I catch up to her, the bus has pulled up.

"Justine?"

She looks at me, surprised, as the bus doors open.

I'm trying to catch my breath because I don't have much time.

"You're my rock."

The bus driver is telling her to get on the bus, but she's just standing there, an I-think-I'm-going-to-cry look on her face. But I grin at her and she grins back.

She gets onto the bus and walks to the back, waving, and I stay there until the bus is out of sight.

I'm about to walk into the house when Will pulls up, so I stop and sit on the step.

He has a relieved look on his face, and I can tell he wants to go into a question frenzy. He squeezes in next to me and we don't say anything for a moment or two.

"Promise me that there will never be another reason for that Tara Finke chick to call me?" he says, taking my hand.

I don't want to, but I laugh, and he leans over and kisses me on the side of my neck and he keeps his face there for a moment.

"I'm sorry," he says, "for that time I kissed you at that party and for that time at the wedding and more than anything for the thousand times that I wanted to and didn't have the guts to."

"And for cutting out next year."

"It was always part of my plan. Before I met you."

"But your decision about going came *after* you met me. That's what I don't understand."

He runs his fingers through his hair, frustrated, confused, everything. "We're supposed to be talking about you and how you're feeling," he says.

"Me's easy. Me got on a train and ended up in Woy Woy. You's difficult. You're planning on puking your way through Europe at a time that I thought you were . . . kind of interested in me."

"Kind of interested in you," he laughs, as if he can't believe what he's hearing. "I'm *kind of interested* in calculus and ancient Roman warfare. You don't use words like *kind of interested* to describe how I feel about you."

"You always say it's complicated," I say, turning to face him. "Make it simple for me."

He thinks about it for a moment.

"Okay." He has that calculating-a-math-problem thing written all over his face.

" 'Simple' is breaking up with my girlfriend. I thought it would be much more complicated but it wasn't. I wish I had done it earlier, but there were tons of reasons, logical ones, for going out with her. Everything was *nice*. Not dramatic, not emotional, not feeling like a yo-yo or comparing someone you're crazy about to stationery, it was just nice. I'd look at her and think, nice. Nice body, nice face, sex would be nice. . . ."

"Will," I interrupt. "Do I need to hear the 'sex would be nice' stuff? I had a bit of a mini-breakdown yesterday and you're not cheering me up."

"Yes you do, because breaking up with her was so easy and breaking up with you would be like, I don't even want to think about it."

"We haven't even started going out together and you're thinking of breaking up."

"But that's it. When I think of you, I think of future stuff. I think of *this is it* and I'm not supposed to think *this is it* at my age. I don't look at you and think *nice*. I look at you and think, oh my God, I want to hold her and never let her go. I think, sex—right here, right now—"

"Frankie!"

My dad is behind us and Will swings around in shock, instantly getting onto his feet and staring up at my father, who is glaring.

"We'll be leaving in five minutes," he says, eyeing Will.

"Papa, this is Will."

My father nods, taking in every detail, and then he goes inside. Will sits down, stunned.

"He heard the sex bit."

"If you said the word 'sex' to me and I was standing a thousand miles away from him, he'd hear it."

I laugh, because I can't help it. I can't believe I'm talking about having sex, and I know this sounds slack, but I just love it when Will's all confused and rambling.

"Am I making sense?" he asks.

"Weirdly enough, yes."

"Last year on Reflection Day we had to write down what our foundations were and whether we thought they were strong enough to get us through unfamiliar territory, and I thought, shit no. Go overseas and have my whole world back here change? No way. I didn't even know who I was *here,* so what made me think that I'd know who I was over *there?*

"But we had to do the list again this year, so I went for it. I didn't put down Sebastian's, because school's not going to be there next year, nor is being a prefect or choirboy or rugby loser or anything else. And that freaked me out, because I wondered, what am I if I'm not all those things? But I stuck to three truths. The first is that my family loves me. It's unconditional, and I know this because of the way they've dealt with things in my older brothers' lives that they don't believe in but support. Secondly is that I'm good at building things, and thirdly is how I feel about you, but more than anything how I feel about me because of you.

"Sometimes you look at me and it's like all the bullshit gets stripped off and I'm left with what's underneath and I kind of like what I see. Someone who actually fails. Someone who has absolutely no self-control. Someone who says real dickhead things like 'this is complicated.' I like that part of me, you know. I like the fact that I know I can't control you or how I feel about you and that doesn't freak me out."

"I love it when you're demented like this."

He's unstoppable. "But sometimes I get terrified and think that everything may change and I won't know where to fit in when I get back, after I've spent a whole lifetime fitting in. Or what if that dickhead Mackee and that psycho Hailler grow a brain and you start finding yourself attracted to them, if you aren't already?"

"If you stay behind, the whole change thing might happen anyway," I tell him. "The not-fitting-in stuff. Certainly not the part about me being attracted to Thomas and Jimmy."

He kisses me softly and just stares. I get a bit embarrassed because it's so intense.

"What are you looking at?" I ask.

"Why, I'm looking at you, miss."

Oh my God. He's quoting a romantic scene out of *The Last of the Mohicans*.

"I thought you only watched it for the massacres," I say, grinning.

"I watched it again. Although you can't go past that last scene when he guts that guy."

"Oh, I think I can."

We laugh for a moment.

"Thank God for e-mail, right?" he says. "It's not that far when you think about it."

I shake my head.

"Write me letters, Will. Write me long letters."

I feel sad. No matter what he's said, I still feel sad and I want to cry because I'm losing him at a time that I've actually found him.

"If I asked you to stay, would you?" I ask later as we're standing by his car.

"Maybe I would, but I don't think you'd ask me. But I swear to God that I'll be on the first plane back if you ever need saving from anything. . . ."

I shake my head again.

"You go and shake your foundations, Will. I think it's about time I saved myself."

Chapter 34

IT'S ALMOST THE end of term three and the Year Twelves are on their way out. I can't believe that my senior year is about to begin, but I'm looking forward to it, despite Will going and even with my mum the way she is. I stand talking to Will and without thinking, we're holding hands. Mr. Brolin approaches us and puts us on detention for breaking the "hands-off" policy, and while he's writing in our diaries, we're killing ourselves laughing, which makes him angrier.

Later, I'm standing in the middle of the courtyard, just watching everyone.

I love this school. I love how uncomplicated it is and the fact that we come from almost two hundred suburbs, so we have to work hard at finding something to hold us together. There's not a common culture or social group. There's a whole lot of individuality, where it doesn't matter that we're not all going to be heart surgeons and it doesn't matter whether you sing in a choir, or play a piano accordion, or lose dismally at rugby league, or are victorious in basketball. I remember a poem we're studying. I think it's Bruce Dawe. About constants in a world of variables. That's what this place is, I guess. And it might be mundane, but I think I need the constant rather than the variable at the moment.

"A good day or a shocker?" Mr. Ortley joins me.

"A good one. There've been a few in a row now."

"The music department is going to do a musical next year," he tells me, rolling his eyes like I would.

Justine is running toward me, and I can tell by the look on her face that she's found out about the musical, too.

I sigh, shaking my head. "I have to give Justine a lesson in holding back," I tell him. "She's just way too enthusiastic."

She grabs my arms in excitement.

"We're doing *Les Mis.*"

I scream hysterically, clutching her as we jump up and down.

Siobhan and Tara walk toward us. "You guys are so uncool. I don't know why we hang out with you," Siobhan says.

Justine and I do a medley of songs for them, and then we listen to Tara explain the conspiracy theory behind her being elected one of next year's leaders.

"They want to control me," she tells us.

Siobhan looks at me over Tara's head and I can't help laughing.

"How will Thomas feel about that?" I ask.

"What's that supposed to mean?"

I shrug. "That night for my birthday, I thought I saw something happening between you two."

Siobhan looks at Tara, stunned.

"No way," Siobhan says, mouth gaping open.

"Can I remind everyone that a day after that event Francesca schized out, so let's presume she was imagining things."

"But your face is red at the moment," Justine says.

"I'm not having this discussion. Thomas Mackee is the last bastion of arrested development and hormonal retardation."

"Sometimes he can be really deep," Justine says.

Thomas bulldozes past and grabs Tara under his arm and drags her away, almost hanging upside down.

"Tom!" she snaps.

She disentangles herself and walks back to us, trying to fix up her uniform.

"Shut up," she says at the faces we're making.

And then I stop.

I stop laughing and I stop walking. My heart is in my mouth and somehow I'm crying and I just can't hold back.

"Francesca?" They hover around me. "What is it?" they ask, clutching at my arm. People grab me. Justine is distressed. Will's there and Thomas is there and Eva Rodriguez and Jimmy.

I pull myself together and take a deep breath.

"My mum's here," I whisper to them, wiping my face with the back of my hand. "My mum's here to pick me up."

A guy walks by us and I can tell he's overheard me. "I don't understand girls," he tells his friends. "They have to get emotional about everything."

I'm crying and laughing at the same time, and the next minute Luca is flying past me.

"Come on, Francesca. What are you waiting for?" he shouts, almost jumping the fence.

She looks pale, but she manages to smile and tries hard to make conversation. Luca and I fill in the spaces but sometimes I think there are just too many to fill, and I can see the way she looks at her surroundings as we drive through the suburbs. Like she's been gone for a long time and doesn't know how to get back. When we get home, the people across the road wave, and I wave back.

And that night we lie on my parents' bed and my dad's snoring and I'm telling my mum about the Tara conspiracy and at the same time Luca is telling her about the trip they're taking to Canberra next term and I tell him that I started my story first and to wait and he says that he has to go to bed earlier so he should finish his first and my dad wakes up for a moment and bellows, "Go to bed," and then there's silence and the snoring begins again and we start speaking again and my mother says, "What is this, Grand Central Station?"

Chapter 35

THIS MORNING, MY mother got out of bed.

She's not up to a pep talk, but the day began with a song at 6:45. Today it was Natalie Merchant's "Kind and Generous." When I questioned her choice, she said it was random, but I know that it was a subliminal way of telling us how she felt.

One thousand questions went through my mind. Just say I got home this afternoon and nothing'd changed? Just say this was one good day out of a thousand bad ones? Just say Luca and my dad and I weren't enough to keep those black days away?

I brushed my teeth and on the mirror in front of me there was one of those motivational messages.

Do something that scares you every day.

I looked at it for a long time.

And for the first time all year I went to school with hope in my heart.

about the author

MELINA MARCHETTA'S first novel, *Looking for Alibrandi*, swept the pool of Australian literary awards for young adult fiction in 1993, winning the Children's Book Council of Australia Book of the Year Award (Older Readers), the Multicultural Book of the Year Award, the Kids Own Australian Literature Award, and the Variety Club Young People's category of the 3M Talking Book of the Year Award. It was also highly commended in the New South Wales Family Therapy Award and in 1996 was short-listed for the prestigious German Prize for Youth Literature. It also won the 2000 Fairlight Talking Book Award for the most outstanding young people's audiobook in the past ten years.

Looking for Alibrandi was released as a major Australian film in 2000, and the screenplay, written by Melina, won an AFI Award as well as the New South Wales Premier's Literary Award and the Film Critics Circle of Australia Award.

Melina lives in Sydney. She is also the author of the Printz Award winner *Jellicoe Road*.